HOW TO GET LUCKY

LAUREN BLAKELY

JOE ARDEN

LITTLE DOG PRESS

DEDICATION

For the readers and listeners! We couldn't do this without you!

Lauren & Joe

ALSO BY LAUREN BLAKELY

Big Rock Series

Big Rock

Mister O

Well Hung

Full Package

Joy Ride

Hard Wood

The Guys Who Got Away Series

Dear Sexy Ex-Boyfriend

The What If Guy

Thanks for Last Night

The Gift Series

The Engagement Gift

The Virgin Gift

The Decadent Gift

The Extravagant Duet

One Night Only

One Exquisite Touch

MM Standalone Novels

A Guy Walks Into My Bar

One Time Only

The Heartbreakers Series

Once Upon a Real Good Time

Once Upon a Sure Thing

Once Upon a Wild Fling

Boyfriend Material

Special Delivery

Asking For a Friend

Sex and Other Shiny Objects

One Night Stand-In

Lucky In Love Series

Best Laid Plans

The Feel Good Factor

Nobody Does It Better

Unzipped

Always Satisfied Series

Satisfaction Guaranteed

Instant Gratification

Overnight Service

Never Have I Ever

PS It's Always Been You

The Sexy Suit Series

Lucky Suit

The Pretending Plot (previously called *Pretending He's Mine*)

The Dating Proposal

The Second Chance Plan (previously called *Caught Up In Us)*

The Private Rehearsal (previously called *Playing With Her Heart*)

Seductive Nights Series

Night After Night

After This Night

One More Night

A Wildly Seductive Night

ABOUT

A sexy standalone romance written by #1 NYT Best-selling Author Lauren Blakely and Award-Winning Romance Narrator Joe Arden!

Every man knows there are lines you don't cross. Like this one -- don't bang your boss's little sister.

Too bad I didn't know sexy, clever, irresistible London is related to the guy who signs my paychecks. Would have been helpful to have that intel before I took her out on that first date, before I kissed her on the beach, before I made plans to take her home that night.

But now I know and I'm going to be so damn disciplined. I'm a good guy, after all. And good guys don't break the golden rules of the bro code. I'm going to follow the heck out of all the rules. I won't break a single damn one.

Even when London asks me to help her with a work project. One that has us working late every night, all alone, in my tiny apartment.

One that tests every ounce of willpower I have.

One that is driving me out of my ever loving mind. But I resist.

Until the night she issues a challenge I can't refuse.

HOW TO GET LUCKY

By Lauren Blakely and Joe Arden

Want to be the first to learn of sales, new releases, preorders and special freebies? Sign up for Lauren's VIP mailing list here!

PROLOGUE

I don't have to see something to believe it. Don't have to experience something to know I'd like it.

I've never vacationed in Fiji, for instance, but I'm 100 percent confident I'd love every second in that tropical paradise.

I don't need to have tossed out the ceremonial first pitch at Dodger Stadium to know that it would be an all-time highlight if I did.

And there's one more thing.

I don't need to have had great sex to know I'd love it.

I'm confident I'd absolutely completely fucking adore, worship, and revere it.

But much like zip-lining in Costa Rica or being front row at a Red Hot Chili Peppers concert, great sex is an incredible life event that I know exists. It's just one I've never experienced.

Not that I haven't had sex at all. Far from it. I just haven't had that toe-curling, leg-shaking kind I've heard so much about. And I have heard about it because I listen. But all that listening hasn't translated into great sex.

Yet.

And that's not due to a lack of enthusiasm on my part. I'd happily enter a booty boot camp, take a coitus crash course or a lovemaking master class, and study until I've got this thing dialed in.

But I haven't had the chance.

Which is a head-scratching travesty, but it happens, okay?

Like, if you get involved in a long-term relationship with a woman who's only into sex every other Saturday night, and who only wants missionary and only with the lights off.

That last rule of the bedroom with my ex was bumpy to navigate. Because light is awesome, what with the way it illuminates the female form and all its curves, dips, and delicious valleys.

Also, what the hell was up with the nighttime-only law? I'm sure I'd be super into afternoon delights.

Morning bangs too. My dick certainly seems interested in the a.m.

But, hey, I loved her, so I went along with the pencil-in-sex-on-the-calendar approach.

Twice a month was better than, God forbid, the Gobi Desert of once every four weeks.

Or worse, the vast arctic wasteland of once a year.

My thoughts and prayers go out to all the dudes suffering from birthday-only boinking.

But I know that sex shouldn't be on a schedule. Not unless the schedule is part of the foreplay, like sending dirty daytime texts to your partner about what you're going to do at ten o'clock sharp when you're mad with desire after a full day spent apart.

That kind of planning is hella sexy.

And sex shouldn't be in the same position every time. It should be imaginative.

It should be raw.

And I'm pretty damn sure sex should be fun.

You know what's *not* fun?

Finding my girlfriend and the dog walker bringing new meaning to the phrase *doggie style*.

At least they weren't using a leash. Poor guy needed his exercise, and all he was doing was chasing his tail while the ex was giving hers away.

They say good guys finish last, but I don't believe that. When a good guy finds the right woman, they can both finish. *Together.* A lot.

So, here I am, twenty-eight, single AF, and ready to find that right woman. One who'll practice with me until perfect and then practice some more—every position, kink, and dirty deed.

My luck is due for a change. And when a sexy, sweet, sarcastic brunette walks into my life, it feels like I'm holding the winning lottery ticket and all I can think is *Yes, yes, yes, it's about fucking time.*

Then, I find out who she is.

And, yeah, she *is* sexy, sweet, and sarcastic. But she is also *100 percent forbidden*.

Which means I'm back to square one.

Until the night she issues me a challenge I can't refuse.

1

The bass pulses through the dressing room. The fluorescent lights flicker overhead as a water bottle next to the mirror vibrates in time with the sound of JT promising to bring sexy back. It's a reminder that in about one hundred twenty seconds, *my ass* needs to be back in the booth.

If only Stanley could make up his mind.

Heaving a sigh, he scratches his chin. "I dunno. Am I feeling 'Hot for Teacher' tonight, or 'School's Out for Summer'?"

Indecision, thy name is Stanley the Entertainer. *Not* his stage name.

"Can't go wrong with 'Hot for Teacher,'" I say. He picks that tune 66 percent of the time. I've done the math.

He tilts his head back and forth like he's deeply torn. And he is. "But, T-man, I also dig the Alice Cooper tune."

Here's a backstage secret from Edge: the long-haired, super-jacked, inked, and bearded dancer is a mild-mannered, soft-spoken marshmallow.

WHO CANNOT PICK HIS SONGS.

"Want me to pick for you?" I ask, keeping my voice nice and calm.

His face lights up, like I've given him free pizza for life. "Dude, would you? That'd be so chill."

Um, yeah, I pick every time he can't choose. "No problem, man."

Stanley draws a couple of deep breaths, psyching himself up before he hits the stage here as Professor Bulge. As I like to say sometimes when I intro him, his PhD stands for Pleasing Her Deeply and he graduated cum louder.

He checks the buttons on his breakaway khakis as Sam bursts through the doors. "Woo-hoo. Gentlemen, it is hot out there tonight. Brittney is turning forty, and Mama is frisky."

He grabs a towel and wipes the sweat and oil off his chest. Sam is exactly the kind of guy you'd expect to be one of the stars every weekend at Edge. His six-foot, two-inch frame and box cutter abs scream *male entertainer* so loudly he's actually on the billboard for the club's all-male revue.

Which is a damn good thing, since that billboard draws the crowds. We're talking about a packed joint every Thursday, Friday, and Saturday. When Edge operates as a traditional dance spot the other nights of the week, I do fine, but the revue gets booked months in advance. And since I earn an hourly wage *and* share the tips, I'm all for the signs that display the washboards to bring in the crowds.

"How frisky?" I ask, hoping it's a good night. "Are we talking raining ones or a downpour of twenties?"

Sam scoffs. "Carlos is still out there picking up his greenbacks. But it was like a tropical sun-shower for me, bro. I love when the weather brings in the good stuff."

That's typical Sam—confident but chill. When everything with Tracy and me fell apart a year ago, Sam was there for me. There for late-night burrito runs, Van Damme movie marathons, and a place to live till I found my own unit in the same building. Plus, he snagged me a gig spinning tunes here at Edge, and hell, did I ever need the job.

"What up, teach?" he booms to Stanley, bear-hugging him.

"Hey, buddy, watch the shirt." The burly man smooths the front of his argyle cardigan. "I just had this ironed," Stanley says in mock frustration.

Sam puts his hands on his thighs and purses his lips. "Oh, I'm very sorry, professor. Do you need to see me after class?" he chirps in a terrible imitation of a sexy coed's voice.

"I think we both need to see you put some pants on," I say.

Sam glances down at his yellow spandex boxer briefs, which don't leave much to the imagination, but that's the point. "What's the big deal, dude? I wear the same thing around the building too."

"Yeah, and I'm pretty sure the HOA doesn't list

'banana hammock' as appropriate attire for communal spaces."

Sam claps me on the shoulder. "Mrs. Morales never complains. You're just uptight because you haven't been laid in a year."

"Gee. I hadn't thought of that."

"Wait," Stanley chimes in. "How about we get Teddy a date? I can set up a dating profile for our favorite deejay. I love doing those."

"Not necessary," I say, even though, my God, either of those would be fucking fantastic. A date or sex, that is, not a dating profile.

I tap my wrist to indicate the time. "On that note."

I grab Bulge's glasses from between the hair gel and coconut oil on the dressing room counter and toss them to Stanley. "Don't forget the specs."

He breathes another long sigh of relief. "Songs, glasses . . . What would I do without you, DJ Insomnia?"

"It's a mystery to me too," I say. I head back to the booth, my voice echoing over the loudspeakers as I turn on the mic while Carlos leaves the stage.

"And now, ladies and ladies and, yes, I see some gents too—it's time to put your books away and sharpen those pencils because school is in session. Our next performer earned a bachelor's degree in being a bachelor and a master's in being your master . . . Give it up for Professor Bulge."

And with that, Stanley pushes through the double doors, strobe light and fog hiding his face, and makes his way to the guest of honor as she hoots and hollers from a chair onstage. The dancer locks his hands on the back of birthday Brittney's chair and rides her leg like he's breaking in a prized colt.

Which is the point of his job—to make Brittney feel like the only woman in the room. And he's damn good at it.

Even from my vantage point above the floor, Brittney looks as happy as I am when I find a fresh, new record.

Nearby, her friends cheer like they have megaphones. One of the many things I love about the women who enter Edge is how, while they don't object to the beefcake, they're so clearly here for the camaraderie with their friends. I don't see many sad solo women nursing drinks in corners here.

And I do a lot of observing. Occupational hazard, you might say, but I think of it as a benefit.

I have the time to people-watch, and it's become a favorite pastime of mine—studying human behavior—and few places are better than the fishbowl of a club.

A place where, technically, I could meet plenty of women to ask out on dates. But I haven't.

Because work is work.

And because dating these days is scarier than clowns, dentists, and clown dentists.

As Bulge finishes his dance, he moves around the stage, ripping off his pants and unbuttoning his elbow-patched cardigan. The bills come out. Ladies stuff tens in his spandex briefs or tastefully throw fives on the stage. Over by the bar, a couple of guys do too, laughing happily as they tuck in some greenbacks.

Once Bulge has received his extra credit, one dude

smacks a kiss on the other, then they catch the gaze of the woman with them, who flashes the biggest smile their way.

A bright, gorgeous grin that lights up her face.

Followed by an eye roll that is somehow both adorable and feisty.

And now I'm definitely glad that checking out the guests is in the job description because . . . holy shit. I'm not sure I can look away.

She's like a sexy librarian with her hair piled on her head in a messy bun and adorable red glasses sliding down her nose. Her chestnut curls dance playfully off her cheeks, which have just the slightest hint of red in them, like she's turned on or embarrassed. Or both. Or neither.

Now I wish my only job were to keep my eyes on the patrons, because I could stare at her all night.

But the last notes of Van Halen's "Hot for Teacher" are playing, and that means I'm up.

As the music fades, my voice booms over the PA system. "Professor Bulge has to grade some papers right now, but you'll find him on the side stage in a little while. Right now, I have a very special treat for you. His business is taking care of your business. He's the CAO of the most successful company in LA. It's our Chief Arousal Officer, Mr. Jerkins."

The lights shift, I fade to the next track, and Sam, now in his Mr. Jerkins attire, saunters onto the stage in his tailored suit while Bulge tosses out some detention slips on his way backstage.

Once Mr. Jerkins hits the lights, I take up the cause

again, my eyes hunting for the sexy librarian, but she's nowhere to be seen.

My shoulders sag.

I sigh, run my hand through my hair, and shrug.

But what can you do?

It's not like I was going to jump over the edge of the DJ booth, sidle up, and ask for her number.

I want to keep my job, and hitting on patrons is numero uno on the Do Not Do List at Edge.

It's a short list. House rules are *hands off the guests, the staff, the money*.

Easy as one, two, three. Like the Jackson 5 song.

As the night winds down, I program the next few tracks to play and head to the bar for a refill—water, of course. Seltzer, actually, since I do love my bubbles.

And I'm not alone.

The brunette thanks the bartender and reaches for what looks like a Diet Coke, her friends nowhere to be seen.

As I'm walking to the counter, Aerosmith's "Crazy" hits the chorus, and she spins in her stool, playing air guitar like she's auditioning for the band. Her gaze swings to mine, and I'm instantly lost in the most arresting brown eyes I've ever seen—they're like brandy.

She doesn't miss a beat. Just flashes me a smile and keeps jamming.

I don't know what comes over me. Nothing. Everything. But without thinking, I tell her, "You're in air guitar C, but you want to be in air guitar E for this part."

Her hands freeze. "Perish the thought of playing in

the wrong key," she says, all dry and deadpan.

I'm about to reply when Jake slides my seltzer across the bar. "Here you go, DJ Insomnia."

I whiplash back into the moment—work, I'm at *work* —and that's my cue to go back to fucking work.

Good thing too. Because as much as I want to grab a stool and chat her up, this dude abides by the Do Not Do List.

I've got plans. So many damn plans. And they all start and end with not repeating the mistakes of the past.

So, with that firmly in mind, I head back to my perch to finish out this Saturday night.

Nighttime is my favorite.

It's the vibe I know, the vibe I love. The club always feels a little off when the lights go up, the sounds go down, and the artifice is exposed.

It also means it's time to go.

I turn off the amp, mixer, and computer, then slide my iPhone into my pocket and rap twice on the door to the DJ booth for good luck.

On my way out of the club, I stop by the manager's office, since it's always wise to be on good terms with the guy who signs your paychecks.

Something that *wasn't* always the case at my last gig.

Plus, Archer is a cool cat, even if he likes Coldplay. I can forgive him for that sin, since the rest of his musical taste is top-notch.

When I pop in, he's rocking out to My Chemical Romance, spreadsheets open on his laptop.

I point at the computer speakers. "An excellent choice. I saw them at the Palladium a few years ago. Sick show."

"Love these guys. And glad to have the DJ's approval," he says, leaning back in his chair in that casual manner of his.

"Happy to give it. I'm out of here, but I'll see you in a few days. We've got that double bachelorette party on Thursday, right?"

"We do. Bring your A game. Should be a wild one."

I smile. "You'll only get the best. I have some great new tunes and mixes lined up. I'm pretty sure the hot dancers are the main reason those ladies are coming, but hey, everything is better with a good soundtrack."

"Great, Teddy. Always love hearing the stuff you find. Oh, also," Archer continues, shifting gears, "your one year with the company is coming up next month."

"It's been that long already?" This job has been the best part of a year that started out as a dumpster fire.

"Sounds like a nice time for a raise," he says, lifting his brows, leading the horse to water.

And, oh yes, I will drink that. Not going to turn down some extra cash. "I am a big fan of raises," I say with a smile. I'm tempted to add *sir* in an eager-to-please way, but Archer would roll his eyes, and rightfully so.

I thank him and head out of the club, amped up by the possibility of not just a raise, but of doing everything differently this time around.

2

When most people envision life in Los Angeles, they think of beaches, celebs, and crazy-good food. And they're not wrong. All those things rock.

But for me, one of the best parts of living in Los Angeles is the twenty-four-hour Target.

Do I frequently find myself walking its aisles at three in the morning? No. But when I do need to hit it after my shift ends, all-hours access to Target is awesome.

Plus, I'm amped up tonight. I can't stop thinking about the brown-eyed beauty who seemed interested and not interested at the same damn time.

I turn that over in my head as I park my Prius in between two other Priuses. (Or is it Prii? Whatever it is, there are a lot of 'em in LA.)

Will I see her again?

Seems doubtful.

Best to put her out of my mind.

And since it's pushing one a.m., I make a detour for treats and toys on the way home.

Not for myself, but for my fifty-pound rescue pit bull, David Bowie. I love that gray-and-white ball of muscle. He's the only thing I salvaged after my breakup with Tracy—the only thing that mattered to me.

Bowie happens to be a dog-toy aficionado, so I make my way to the best aisle in the store and load up my red basket with braided rawhides, salmon chews, and a squeaky duck. Bowie mans the home front while I'm putting on the show, so now and then, he gets a reward for his security work. He's excited to see me either way, but I'm sure the treats help. Hell, I like treats. I wouldn't object to someone bringing home treats for me.

I grab some of the store's special home-baked dog biscuits, then I throw a furry hedgehog toy into the basket because it is a truth universally acknowledged that all pooches in possession of a good hedgie must be in want of nothing. Props to Jane Austen for an epic first line in *Pride and Prejudice*—a line which can be applied to pretty much anything.

I buy the toys, head home, and give my boy a hello.

Or really, he greets me with a goofy smile and a face lick.

After I take him outside, I toss him his new stuffed playmate, hit the sack, and put the air guitarist out of my mind.

It's not as if I'm going to see her again.

And if she did come back to the revue, well, that might mean I'm not her type.

Since, ya know, I'm not a stripper. And strippers are generally the reason people frequent the club every weekend when the guys are in all their, as Sam likes to say, *abilicious* glory.

I do have good abs though. I blame LA for that.

Or really, I *thank* LA for that.

And as I hit the hay, I don't think of Miss Air Guitar for one second. Not at all. Not even a little bit.

Women only mean distraction—and I sure as hell don't need that in my life right now.

Ever listen to a song you've never heard before on the radio and then go home and hear that same song on a TV show? Or a commercial?

I have a theory about that.

It's not that everyone in the entertainment industry is listening to the same five songs. Though a lot of them are.

The theory is about synchronicity.

It's happening all the time, all over the world. Meaningful coincidences.

We might not always be aware of it.

But I bet we're walking past the same people every day at the farmers market, the park, the coffee shop.

We don't always notice them though.

Unless, like that song on the radio, that person is already on our mind. I'm already thinking about her. I want to be looking for her.

Evidently I'm looking.

And evidently I'm a lucky fucking guy.

Because my theory proves out Sunday afternoon

when I unleash Bowie and open the gate to the Silverlake Dog Park.

In the corner under the shade of a tree, a woman
with red glasses chucks a tennis ball at a Chihuahua
mix, who takes after it like his feet have wings.

Hello, synchronicity, and thank you very much.

The air guitarist wears a vintage *Beverly Hills, 90210*
T-shirt that says "Senioritis" above a shot of the cast.

Another coincidence—I just started streaming that
show.

What are the odds I'd see her again so soon? Not
only that, but she's obviously a fellow dog lover.

This is the universe making everything easy. She's
not a patron of the club right now. This is neutral
territory. Ergo, it's time for my pooch to earn his
treats.

I look down to enlist my furry wingman to help snag
an introduction, but Bowie spots a pair of playful
huskies and abandons me. Can't say I blame him. My
dude loves the chase. Looks like I'm on my own.

I casually make my way up the dirt hill toward the
wavy-haired brunette I haven't stopped thinking about
since last night.

She's even prettier in the sunlight.

My step turns a little hesitant as I get closer. It's been
a while since I've approached a woman. In the club my
confidence is sky high, but I'm in my element there.
Safe behind the DJ booth, perched aloft, looking down
on the action.

Here I'm just a guy who hasn't been on a date in
almost a year. But that won't change unless I get back

out there, and I'd never forgive myself if I let this opportunity slip by.

Before I can second-guess myself anymore, I'm sharing her shade and making eye contact.

I gesture to the '90s throwback tee she's wearing. "This may be an unpopular opinion, but I always thought Andrea was the cutest one on that show," I say.

She smiles back before reaching down to pick up the tennis ball, a hint of recognition in her eyes, like she's trying to place me. "You're not just a fan of the crew, but of the girl who *never* gets picked first?"

I hold up a hand as if I'm taking an oath. "I am all that. Though technically I'm a new fan. I've only streamed a couple episodes, but I definitely dig the whole glasses-and-curls vibe she has going on," I say, and the brunette gives me a *keep going* nod. "Plus, the show *did* have an epic soundtrack, before that became *the* thing for TV shows."

"So, my shirt is retro, but the show was ahead of its time. Yay me," she says with a playful glint in her eyes.

I grin. "Hard to go wrong with R.E.M., Elvis Costello, and Chris Isaak."

She plucks at the fabric and smiles. "That was the slogan on the other shirt I was going to get. Darn. Should have snagged that one."

"I'd wear that shirt too."

She laughs, and I want to pump a fist. Then she screws up the corner of her lips, studying me. "I saw you at the club last night, didn't I? You were the DJ and erstwhile air guitar expert."

Yes. Pretty sure her remembering me falls under the

heading of Keep Going. So I do. "That's what it says on my business card. Both those things, actually."

"I enjoyed your emceeing."

I try to rein in a grin. Compliments from cute women are the best thing ever. "I was up there doing my best Michael Buffer impersonation."

Her brow knits in confusion. "Who's Michael Buffer?"

"You don't know Michael Buffer? Like, from boxing? Or MMA?" How could she not know who he is?

"Not a huge fan of watching men beat the crap out of each other."

"That's understandable. He's a fight announcer. That's literally all he does. Just announces the start and end of a fight. And he's super famous and super rich for just that. You know 'Let's get ready to rumble'?" I say the catchphrase, but don't perform it. She, on the other hand, dives right in.

"Oh yeah! Let's get rrreeeeaaaadddyyyy—"

I cut her off, bringing my finger to my lips. "No, wait! Stop. You better not say it out loud. He might hear you."

She scans the park, left and right, and drops her voice. "Oh, what? Is he like Candyman or something? Is he going to come through a mirror and get me?"

"It's possible. You can't be too safe."

"Thank you so much for the warning. But it's kind of hard not to say. Don't you think?"

"True," I concede. "It's like 'I'll be back' or 'No, I am your father,'" I say, imitating Arnold and James Earl Jones in turn.

She laughs. "Those weren't bad. So come on, let me hear your Michael Buffer . . ."

I'm pretty sure I'd do anything she asked me to. And I'm adhering to the *keep going* rule I just enacted. "I'll do it for you, but if he hears me and sues for trademark infringement, you're paying the fine."

"Consider it paid. Now proceed." She crosses her arms and gives me a playful *I'm waiting* look. I take a deep breath, when my blue-nose bruiser crashes into my knee. I steady myself, since now is not the time to fall, then I mix it up, meeting the brunette's eyes as I imitate the announcer, saying to my pooch, "*Someone is ready to rumble.*"

My audience of one gives an approving nod, dips a hand in her back pocket, then pretends to fish out some money from her wallet. "For your fine."

"Much appreciated." I mime taking it from her and tucking it into my own pocket before I bend down to give my boy some scratches on the chin. "Hey, big guy. How you doing?"

He pants, then hops over to the teacup dog, gently nuzzles his ear, and flops down on his back. The little dog takes his turn and boxes my guy's ears.

The *90210* fan joins in with the pack moment, stroking Bowie on the chin, and if I didn't have a crush on her already, I would now. Women who love dogs are my kryptonite.

"And who is this adorable fellow?" she asks.

"This is David Bowie. He's super friendly. Got him from the North Central shelter about six years ago. The second he looked up at me with that little streak of white between his eyes and that goofy grin, I was a goner."

Her fingers graze mine as we pet him, and yep, Bowie is getting all the treats in the world tonight. I take back everything I said about his wingman skills. He's showing them all and then some right now.

"I'd be a goner too. He's a doll of a dog, and I love rescue mutts."

Bowie takes off, glancing behind him like he's daring the other guy to follow, and the little dog flies. We stand, and her gaze follows the dogs as they race in circles around the park, her expression saying she's getting a kick out of them getting along.

"Love the name. Are you a Stardust fan?"

"Yeah. I've been trying to get him to answer to Ziggy, but so far, no dice."

"You should try Rebel Rebel," she says.

"Not a bad idea." I test it out to no avail and shrug. "Worth a shot. So, who's the little guy running with the big dogs?"

"That's Mr. Darcy. We come here every Saturday morning and Sunday afternoon. Sometimes he goes to the small-dog side of the park, but even though he's seven pounds, he's convinced he's a German shepherd. Hence, he insists on the big-dog side."

"The man knows his mind. Good for him. Honestly, most tiny dogs bark at Bowie like they've got something to prove, but your little guy has some serious swagger. Of course, when you oversee the entirety of the Pemberley estate, you have to have some confidence."

She sizes me up as I drop a not-so-subtle Austen

reference on her. She seems impressed. Hell, I'm impressed. Go me.

"*Pride and Prejudice* fan?"

I try for a twofer, name-dropping from *Persuasion* too. "Honestly, I'm more of a Captain Wentworth guy myself, but Darcy's doing his thing."

She parks a hand on her hip. "Doing his thing? Fitzwilliam has the money, the attitude, the looks, and the charm."

"But Wentworth is a man's man. Fought for his country, made his own fortune, and even after Anne spurned his advances, he knew his heart and put himself out there for her again. That takes guts. What'd Darcy have to lose? Nothing." I keep going. "He had his whole life plated up for him. And sure, he's technically hot, but in that trust-fund-baby-with-plenty-of-time-to-work-out kind of way. But hey, you obviously dig him because you named your cute pooch after him, and he wears it well, so I get it."

She stares at me bug-eyed, which is still a good look on her. "Yes, *my* Mr. Darcy is definitely doing his thing too and I like it. Also, you've thought this through — the whole Darcy/Wentworth debate," she says, but she's not annoyed. More . . . amused.

"What can I say? It's an important topic."

"Definitely. I like a man who's passionate, especially about books." A smile curves her lips, and all I want to do is keep talking to her.

"Now is probably a great time to tell you I majored in literature. And my dad teaches high school English."

She hums, tapping her chin as Mr. Darcy runs two

circles around her legs, then darts off again. "Now I'm curious. How does a lit major find himself deejaying at an all-male revue?"

"Do you mean did I dream about playing 'Pour Some Sugar On Me' for my half-naked buds when I was in fourth grade?"

"That's the path to DJ-hood, right? Cueing up stripper songs as a grade schooler?"

I bring my hand to my heart and sigh exaggeratedly. "Exactly." But while I could talk about my passion all day, I don't want to come on too strong. So I focus on the question she asked—why am I at Edge? "I started deejaying parties in college, and I was able to turn it into a job when I graduated."

I check out Bowie's whereabouts—near the water fountain scampering with Mr. Darcy—before getting to the still-raw bit. "Then last year, when I needed a new gig, my best friend hooked me up. He works there too, which is dope. You'd think a straight guy might not be into spending his nights with a room full of oiled-up men, but honestly, everyone is super fun to be around. More importantly, what brought you and those two dudes there last night?"

"Those guys are my roommates. Nate and Eli. Though technically they're my landlords, since I rent a little studio—like a mother-in-law pad—off their house. They're insanely fun, but also disgustingly in love, and sometimes I feel like the third wheel."

"You always have your solo career as an air guitarist to fall back on if that friendship band breaks up."

She rolls her eyes. "Shut up. Very funny."

"What? I'm serious. You had some real moves. You do know there are air guitar competitions? I've DJ'd some. We could get you into one."

"That's what I've always wanted. To show off my skills with imaginary instruments," she says as Mr. Darcy arrives to drop off the tennis ball.

"No time like the present to build your burgeoning air guitar career. I'm trying to do the same thing with a DJ business I just started—weddings, bar mitzvahs, and corporate events. Los Angeles is the place to be for that."

"This city does have every form of entertainment under the sun," she says as she reaches to pick up the ball that Mr. Darcy brought over, and I can't help myself. I steal a quick glance at her shapely legs and round ass, painted into that pair of jeans. She is fine. "How long have you lived in LA?"

"My whole life."

She shoots me a skeptical stare as she tosses the ball for her eager pup. "No way. No one is from Los Angeles. Do you, like, get a tattoo or something when you're born here?"

I flash briefly to the Celtic trinity knot ink on my left forearm, covered by my long-sleeve shirt. But this moment calls for levity, so I go a different route.

"You do," I say in mock seriousness as the Chihuahua mix takes off in a blur. "Mine says 'Sun's out, buns out.' I can't show it to you now though."

Her eyes glint in a way that says she'd like to see it another time, and I beam inside. This is working. With a naughty little smile, she asks, "But another time? You'll show it to me another time?"

I shrug, the kind that says *yes, of fucking course*. "I could probably be convinced."

She taps her temple. "Duly noted. I'll try to think of how to be convincing, Mr. Native Angelino. Now, if you've been here your whole life, you must love—"

I jump in to finish her sentence. I know where this is going—same place it usually goes. "Surfing and skate-boarding?"

She hesitates like maybe I caught her. "*Tacos.* I was going to say tacos, obviously. You must love tacos."

"To quote the great Ms. Austen, 'Happiness in marriage is entirely a matter of tacos.'"

"And I believe that's a direct quote too."

"It should be," I say. "Actually, I love all Mexican food. If I could only eat one kind of cuisine for the rest of my life, it'd be Mexican. What about you?"

"Ice cream, of course. What could beat a dessert that encompasses all four food groups?"

"Don't get me wrong—I love a cone, but how does ice cream cover all the food groups?"

"Simple science. Strawberry counts as fruit. Mint is clearly a veggie, because mints are leaves. Bacon ice cream covers protein. And every single scoop is dairy. So there."

I laugh. Deeply. "You win that debate."

"Laugh as much as you choose, but you will not laugh me out of my opinion," she fires back at me, and I can tell she's quoting something.

My brain cycles quickly through options, since the

words feel familiar and I want to get it right. "Is that *Emma*?"

"Nice try. *Pride and Prejudice*," she says, her eyes sparkling like she's having fun with this moment and with me. "I was trying to see how sharp you are. The fact that you even know of the existence of *Emma* is pretty impressive."

I blow on my fingernails casually.

"Honestly, though, if it comes right down to it and we are truly picking one non–ice cream option, like a cuisine forever and ever and into time immortal, I'd have to go with Japanese," she adds. "I'm prepared to marry sushi."

And there it is. The universe dropping a golden opportunity in my lap.

I clear my throat and take a deep, fueling breath. The game is on. "I know a great little sushi spot right on the water in Santa Monica. Have you ever been to Yoshi? I'd love to take you."

And whoa. Did I just ask her out? Yes. Yes, I did.

She pauses, and when she glances at her shoes, I can see her hesitation. She's taking too long to answer.

My stomach plummets.

Finally, she looks up, and her brown eyes sparkle. Something's going on in her head, and boy, do I ever want to know what.

"That actually sounds great. I'd love to. Because I had this great idea. Sort of like a project."

Dear God, please let it be a sex project.

A man can dream.

"Sure. I'm game for projects," I say, trying to sound cool and casual.

"Terrific, but I should probably get your name first. I'm London, like the city." There's a hint of rasp in her voice that makes me hope even harder for a sex project.

And a yes to the date. Of course.

"I'm Teddy, like the bear."

She arches one sexy brow. How the hell is an eyebrow sexy? "Or you could say Teddy, like a lace cami."

It takes me a second to process her innuendo.

One. Hot. Second.

My throat is dry. My skin is sizzling. And my luck is about to change. "That's what I meant to say, and I can't wait to hear about your proposition."

The smile she flashes my way tells me *proposition* was exactly the right word. "Let's drop off our dogs, and I'll meet you at Yoshi tonight at eight?"

"I'm there."

"And I'll tell you all about what I've been thinking," she says with a smile that makes me think, *Yes, I am about to score on all fronts.*

A great date with a cool babe, and then maybe a little something more.

Or a lot something more.

Yep. An urgent need to see me tonight, a lingerie innuendo, and a bit of nervous hesitation when I first asked for the date.

Sex has to be her project.

And she's come to the right guy.

3

That evening

From the Woman Power Trio, aka the text messages of London and her two besties, Olive and Emery

London: Stop the presses. I have a date tonight.

Emery: Listening to a podcast while you ignore our texts is not a date. Even if you do it with a glass of wine.

Olive: Is this the lit one where you geek out to Brontë and Austen deets? Wait, no. Must be that science one where you pretend you're going to date the hottie host. I didn't realize how serious it was, but I suppose when you've listened to every episode . . .

London: WITH A GUY. And I do not ignore you two.

Though, fine, the *Science of Everyday Things* podcast guy does have a hella sexy voice.

Olive: Like my favorite audiobook narrator?

London: We are not discussing your narrator crush right now!

Emery: Yeah, Olive, way to be an attention hog. We are discussing London's *supposedly* real date.

Olive: Yes, tell us everything. Does he meet the four basic requirements? Straight? College-educated? Gainfully employed? And doesn't live at home with his parents? Wait. Amend that—it's hard to live on your own in LA. Let's say, "Doesn't expect his mom to do his laundry."

London: Pretty sure he's ticking all of the above boxes. As in, he has his own place. I bet he does his own laundry too.

Emery: Le sigh. He's not real, then.

Olive: I know. He's soooo not real. Take a pic. Prove it.

London: I'm not taking a pic of my date. But I will say we had mega spark.

Olive: Spark is gooooood.

Emery: Spark is necessary.

London: Spark is what I didn't have for so long. And this guy is all spark. He's scrumptious, with hazel eyes and sandy-brown hair, all sun-kissed and golden, and a stubbled jawline. He's edible and funny and clever, and . . . HE LOVES DOGS.

Emery: Yup. Imaginary.

Olive: So imaginary. But tell us where you're going just in case we need to save you. Or spy on you.

London: Yoshi. In Santa Monica.

Olive: On the beach. Nice.

London: If you spy, don't be creepy.

Emery: *rolls eyes* Don't be silly. We *only* spy creepily.

Olive: By the way, we want a full report tomorrow.

Emery: Unless you're banging him. Then give us the report post-banging.

London: There will be no banging tonight. But I'm not opposed to . . . other things. Even though I have a project for him.

Olive: I bet you do.

London: I swear. It's a work thing.

Olive: Wink, wink. Have fun with your *work thing*.

4

London is a choreographer.

She spent three years in Vegas.

She's been back in Los Angeles for two weeks.

All of which I've learned in the first thirty minutes of our date, since I like listening to her and I want to get to know her.

Also, synchronicity has to be in play again. Because her being a professional choreographer totally works for me. After all, what's a DJ without some dancing?

After the waiter brings appetizers and drinks to our table on the patio, we pick up the banter as if we never hit pause when we left the dog park. I take another pull of my beer and reach for a warm salted edamame while the ocean breeze brushes my shoulders and the surf crashes in the distance.

"I'm always curious about places like Vegas. Spots where people vacation and visit. What's it like working and living there?"

"I liked it for the most part. But Vegas is also . . ." She

doesn't complete the thought immediately, just pauses with an edamame midair then finishes, "*Complicated.* Still not sure if Sin City and I are done, but we definitely needed a break."

Sounds like there's more to that story, but I don't want to press yet, so I file away the *complicated* for a later conversation as she eats the edamame.

"I've only been to Vegas twice, and I can definitely say that a weekend always felt like the right amount of time for a visit," she says.

"Do you like downtown or the Strip?"

"My first trip was for a friend's bachelor party, and we stayed at Aria. But the last time, Sam and some other guys and I stayed down on Fremont, and that was definitely more my scene. Kinda dive-y, kinda dirty, but in a good way. And lots of fun clubs and bars with great music."

"Always a plus, Mr. Music. My work was on the Strip, so that's where I spent most of my time, but whenever I had a night off, downtown was where I'd be. You've got me thinking about traveling now though. Love a good road trip."

"We should totally make that happen. California is the best road trip state." The second that sentence is out of my mouth, it feels like I might be coming on too strong. But at the same time, I could see myself taking a road trip with her, spending a long weekend in San Francisco maybe. I can picture it, and I like what I see.

"I could be into that," she says, pulling me from my thoughts and putting another huge smile on my face. But we haven't even made it to green tea ice cream yet, so I try to pump the mental brakes. I focus on getting the conversation back on her.

"Did you always want to choreograph?"

She adjusts her red glasses. "At first, I wanted to be a scientist."

I hold up a hand. "Wait. Scientist?"

"Geek here," she says, patting her sternum. "I was a full-on science nerd as a kid. Beakers, make-your-own-volcano kits, periodic table coloring book—the whole nine yards."

"Naturally, you went from microscopes to dance," I say.

"Of course. It's a normal segue for a grade schooler," she deadpans. "I still love science, and I'm addicted to *The Science of Everyday Things*."

"That podcast? I've heard it's good. Been meaning to check it out."

Her eyes light up with delight. "You have to. It's sooo good. The episode on how credit card readers work was kind of mind-blowing."

I tap my temple. "Mental note made."

"But as much as I love science, I loved dance a little more growing up. When I discovered it, I ditched my lab coats for leotards. I wanted to dance professionally. I trained my whole life doing modern. But I had this great dance mentor at Montclair in Jersey. You know the type? One of those people who can kind of see into your soul?"

I picture one of my music teachers from college. "I definitely know the type. They're awesome, but terrifying."

"Yes, that's exactly what Professor Kambara was like," London says, her brown eyes sparkling. "She saw something in me, and I think it was that I was in my head a lot. I was always critical of my own work and my routines. She pulled me aside and asked if I wanted to codirect the spring production, because it turns out my analytical approach was actually ideal for choreography. Funny thing though—at first, I turned her down."

"Why?" I ask, drawn into this story, drawn into her. "Because when you talk about it, you kind of light up."

She dips her face as her lips curve into a grin, maybe a touch embarrassed, but thoroughly adorable. "Thank you. I said no then because I was nineteen and insecure. I figured Professor Kambara didn't think I could hack it as a dancer and was trying to push me away from my passion. I had one lonely night in my dorm with a pint of Cherry Garcia, then Nate knocked on the door."

"Nate as in Nate and Eli?"

Her grin grows wider. "Yes. Good memory."

I give myself a virtual pat on the back.

"He insisted on sharing the pint and listening to why I was in a funk. I did both, and he said something wise and pithy like 'You're an asshole if you don't take chances.'"

I laugh. "Yes, that is wise and pithy. Also, true."

She shrugs happily. "I took a chance. Gave it a try. And it was life," she says, drawing out the last word, clearly enjoying the memory.

"I love basically everything about that story, except for one tiny detail." I hold up my thumb and forefinger to show a sliver of space.

"What's that?"

"The food choice. I prefer to do my deep thinking with a bowl of Cinnamon Toast Crunch."

She gives a playfully stern shake of her head. "I have to disagree. Nothing beats B & Js."

I can't help myself. "That's true. Everyone loves good BJs. I know I do."

A laugh bursts from her as she quirks one eyebrow —that damn sexy one again. Though, in all fairness, both are sexy. *All* of her is sexy. "Do you now? How much do you love them?"

I can't answer right away, because I'm pretty much on fire from those words on her pretty lips. "More than I love Prince's 'Purple Rain.'"

"The song or the movie?"

"Both."

"High praise." It comes out flirty, borderline dirty.

It takes everything in my power not to jump across this table and cover her mouth with mine. This woman is hot. And clever. And easy to talk to. Plus, she gives such good flirt.

I take a sip of my Asahi to cool down and return to her story so she doesn't think I'm a sex-crazed maniac with a one-track mind. "So, you put your ego aside, took your friend's advice, and it worked out," I prompt.

"Everything clicked—all of a sudden, my work had no physical limits. With choreography, the only ceiling is my imagination." She picks up another edamame, pops it from the pod, then into her mouth, and when she finishes chewing, says, "But enough about me. I want to hear about you. I truly enjoyed your 'emceeing' last night," she says, sketching air quotes. "But especially your song picks. They were spot on. Then I learned you weren't a fourth-grade DJ prodigy, and I was shocked."

"Yes, it remains shocking to me as well." I shift to a more earnest tone. "But honestly, I've had a similar experience with deejaying. I could never master an instrument the way I wanted, but I was cool with that because I love putting music together even more. Devouring it, experiencing it, sharing it. All genres, all eras, which is why I love doing any kind of event—corporate, weddings, what have you. I've done a few, but nothing serious. It's what I want to do under my own banner, with my own business. It's what I do, too, with a weekly radio show I have. Playing other people's music, at the right time, in the right order, can be its own form of expression." I laugh lightly. "That probably sounds corny, right?"

Or maybe not. Because the way she's locked onto me while I'm talking makes me feel like I'm the only guy in the room—hell, the only guy in the world.

And this date is nothing like the ones I went on with Tracy. London is nothing like my ex. Maybe, just maybe, my luck is changing. Hell, what are the chances the first woman I've asked out since my ex skewered me would be so fucking dope?

I could never have imagined my Sunday night going this well. But hey, synchronicity. It's my turn. I'm going to enjoy this great date, and maybe soon it'll lead to all that great sex.

She jumps in, answering my question. "It does not

sound corny. It sounds awesome. You know what else sounds awesome?"

I lean in, eager to hear. "What's that?"

"That yellowtail you were hyping earlier. And it looks like it is heading this way." Her eyes drift past my shoulder, and I follow her gaze to the sashimi, sushi, and rolls on a porcelain boat that a server carries toward us. He sets the tray down, we thank him, then London and I both go straight for the wasabi to add to our soy sauce. Nice to see I'm not the only one here who likes it hot.

"You like sushi with your wasabi, I see," I say dryly as she drowns the fish and rice in the good green stuff.

"I like it hot, and I'm not afraid to admit it," she says, then leans to the right, rooting around in her little purple purse, fishing for something. She dangles her keys, and I grin like a fool.

"I have one too," I say, grabbing my key ring to show her the mini bottle of sriracha on it.

She drops her voice. "Is yours real though?"

I laugh, like that's the craziest thing I've heard. "Yes, London, it's real." I add in a whisper, "Want a hit? Also, why are you asking if it's real when you have one too?"

"Mine's purely decorative," she says, setting the keys back in her purse as I put mine in my pocket.

I wiggle my fingers for her to fess up. "You're going to need to explain the nonfunctional sriracha bottle. Because . . . why? Sriracha is better than almost any hot sauce anywhere."

"I couldn't agree more. But there are risks in life you take—like choreographing a new show—and risks in life you don't take—like the chance of sticky red goop spilling all over your purse."

"Sure, I get that. But I could argue—lip balm, lipstick, mascara. Those all go in purses too. They could also spill."

Her mouth falls open. She shakes her head, whip fast. "First, the risk of lipstick spillage is smaller than the risk of hot sauce spillage. Second, those are necessities and worth the risk."

"I could argue sriracha is a necessity. Much like wasabi," I say casually, popping a piece of yellowtail into my mouth. "Also, why do you have a decorative bottle? Is it to pledge allegiance to the alliance of sriracha love?"

"Obviously. Also, it's a good luck charm. My brother gave it to me for fun, and the day he did, I snagged the job in Vegas."

"I suspect it was talent that nabbed you the job, but I wholly support homages to the gods and goddesses of luck."

"Gods *and* goddesses. I like that inclusive spirit, Teddy." Her eyes lock with mine, and holy hell. The spark in them is doing things to me. As in, *all the things*.

"Also, you *get* me," she says, still holding my gaze. "You clearly get me."

Oh, do I ever want to get her.

In pretty much every way.

Is this what it's like to feel instant attraction? Perfect chemistry?

If it is, I am all in for both.

Throughout the meal, we talk a little more about

luck, then dive into all things nerd, from *Star Wars* to Adult Swim.

As she plucks at pieces of tuna, snapper, and eel, I notice her chopsticks game is on point, and I can't help thinking of how good her nimble fingers might be at holding something else, much thicker than a chopstick.

Obviously.

I snag another piece of fish off the plate and take stock of this moment. I don't want to forget any of it—the cool beach breeze, the way her face dances in the candlelight on this patio, the one freckle under her right eye that I want to trace with my tongue.

Note to self: find my passport when I get home because I want to spend some time in London.

An unexpectedly wet noise breaks my reverie. It's coming from a couple at a nearby table. London and I snap our gazes to them at the same time.

Because . . . holy loudest lip-smacking ever.

We're talking full-on face-suck.

I lean closer and whisper, "Is it just me, or is he trying to Hoover her whole face?"

She cringes but laughs too. "I hope we'd try a soft butterfly kiss first. That'd be my suggestion."

And I like that suggestion.

In principle.

Not for them though. For her and me.

A few tables away from us, the man's hands slide to the back of the woman's neck and he tilts his head a bit, angling for more. He twists his tattooed hand in her long, straight dark hair, tugging on her locks. If he's not careful, he'll get them caught in his bracelets. Guy must think he's Johnny Depp.

They show no sign of letting up. "Should I let them know?" I ask. "Offer them a tip or something?"

"No. I kind of like to observe," she says, like it's a naughty confession.

And it's one that interests me very much. "You like to observe strangers kissing?"

She shrugs with a smile. "Why not? If they're going to kiss in public, I'm going to exercise my right to observe. Ooh. Look. He's going for a lizard kiss."

I steal a glance. My eyes pop. The guy's tongue is flicking snakelike into his date's mouth. But they don't seem to care. "Mmm, that seems a little animalistic for dinner. Personally, I'd have to recommend the earlobe kiss. Great starter kiss at a restaurant. Sophisticated without being too over-the-top."

London's eyes turn heated, like she's intrigued. *Very intrigued.* "That's your recommendation for kissing choreography?"

"Yes. It's not too PDA-y, but definitely could leave her wanting more." We both seem to have forgotten about the hipster couple and have locked firmly onto each other. At this moment, I've forgotten everything else in my life too. My business plans, the raise . . . all that melts away, and I only feel this burning desire to connect with this woman. Honestly, emotionally and physically.

And right now, the physical is front and center in my mind. "But, of course, I'd welcome your opinion, as a professional choreographer," I add.

"Since you asked, I'd want to know . . . what exactly would that earlobe kiss feel like? I mean, if you had the chance to try it out on a date." Her tone is soft, even more inviting than before. "Say, after sushi, on a dimly lit patio."

I move closer, my voice barely above a whisper. "It would probably feel something like this."

5

I bring my face near hers, our cheeks grazing. Her breath catches as my lips make their way across her jaw. Gently, I kiss along the top of her ear, nuzzling my nose into her hair. I inhale her scent, like freshly peeled oranges, as I kiss delicately along the outside of her ear. I take the lobe into my mouth and suck gently as she exhales on a soft moan, letting me know she's into this as much as I am. I file that intel away—how she murmurs when I kiss here right there.

Let's see if she likes *this*—I bury my nose in that perfect spot behind her ear where her hair meets her neck and give her a firm kiss and a soft bite. Not enough to leave a mark, but enough to let her know I *want* to leave one.

I linger a second longer, cupping her face with my other hand, breathing with her. Her skin prickles, my heart races, and I lean back to take her in. Her eyes glimmer with the first sparks of lust. Her lips part the slightest bit.

She looks blissed out. I feel the same.

After another heady moment where the air between us is still charged, she takes a drink of water, pushing her glasses up on the bridge of her nose. "That's pretty good. I suspect if you did that on a date, the woman would find it very . . . *tasteful*."

"Good to know. Also, maybe she'd find it . . . hot?" I ask, going fishing.

She nibbles on the corner of her lips, her cheeks flushing. "She would."

My pulse spikes, and *yes, yes, yes*. My luck is all changing tonight. "Hopefully that opportunity will present itself one day."

"I hope so too . . ."

But before I can even entertain the idea of trying another kiss on her, our server returns to clear our plates. We order a green tea ice cream to split, and I hope that dessert never arrives because I could sit here with her all night.

She drums her fingers on the table, then draws a deep breath. "I wanted to tell you, Teddy, that I'm having a great time. But . . ."

My stomach plummets like a weight, sinking me. Nothing good can follow *but*.

"I hope this isn't too presumptuous, and I feel like I've been kind of forward with the flirting, and . . ." She stops, an apology crossing her warm brown eyes, and that look sinks me a little further. "And the kissing." She stops again, flapping her hand in front of her face like she's waving away the awkward.

I wish her success with that because I want it gone

too. I have no clue where she's going with this except *no place good*.

"Which I really liked," she adds in a rush, and her tone sounds legit.

She doesn't seem like she's dealing me a line. An *it's not you, it's me* send-off.

Everything about her vibe feels real.

I want to convince myself that's a good sign, but *liked*, as in past tense, isn't what I want with London. I don't want there to be anything past tense about our kissing. Or any kind of tense.

But . . .

"And that's my worry," she says, a little more professional maybe. Distant, even. "Because I got ahead of myself, focusing just on the date part. Which I completely want and wanted. I'm having so much fun with you, and I think you're so great, but I also did want to talk to you about a project. And I don't want to forget in the midst of all that kissing."

That *should* make me feel better.

But it doesn't.

"Right. The project," I say evenly. I don't want to let on that I'd hoped it would be a sex project. It's probably something miserable involving PowerPoints or spreadsheets or other shit I hate. Like maybe she wants me to make a spreadsheet of all her favorite music.

I like London, and I'll do a lot for a woman I'm into, but I draw the line at spreadsheets.

She smiles widely, going for the close. "See, I thought we could pair up, because I'm working for the club too."

I flinch.

What did she just say?

"You work for the club?" Each word comes out occupying its own real estate.

Because this is Road Runner dropping the anvil and then painting the tunnel on the brick wall. And I just ran smack into it.

She works for the club, and that means hands off.

Hands all the way off.

Because of the Do Not Do List.

It's a code that matters to me. It's one I want to abide by and honor.

"Just on a contract basis, but yes." Excitement trips through her tone, the same enthusiasm I heard when she first spoke about her professor, the sign that she loves what she does. "I'm going to be working on a new female dance show for Edge to start out on Wednesday nights. The partners that own the club have had so much success with the male revue, they want to see if they can bring the same fun and energy with female dancers, but not in a revue style. No stripping—sort of like background dancing. Think more Cirque du Soleil than Spearmint Rhino, but still a little sexy," she adds with heat in her eyes.

This is all news to me. I'm surprised Archer hasn't mentioned it. "Sounds interesting," I say.

"I have some ideas I'm *so* excited about, and you're great with music. I always like to make sure I've got the perfect music, and it's good to work with experts. And you seem to know just the right songs for the right moment. I have some epic moves planned and some super-sexy numbers, and the whole thing is going to be fire."

"Sure, sounds great," I say, doing my best to stay enthused.

Because, hey, this is good. It has to be good. The better the club does, the better I can do. Besides, working with London could be . . . fun.

Challenging too, since I'd probably be turned on the entire fucking time. But sure, fun.

"Would you be willing to help me out? I can pay you," she says, her voice pitching up, maybe with nerves.

I shake my head, dismissing that notion. "I'm happy to help." I'm not going to take money from her, especially since she's an employee too. I need to help. I *should* help.

The smile that lights her face almost makes my disappointment worthwhile. She looks gorgeous like this. Happy, animated, pursuing her passion.

Maybe we can simply hit pause on the kissing.

Pick it up where we left off once her contract is up.

"Thank you," she says. "I've been looking for the right person, and you're perfect. So perfect I could kiss you."

Well . . . maybe one more for the road.

"If you insist," I say offhand, like she won't really take me up on it.

"Do you *want* me to insist on it?" The question comes out both flirty and shy.

Like she wants the kissing and the work project.

All I want right now is another kiss.

And it seems we're on the same page, since she sets

her glasses on the table and leans across it. And I'm leaning right back, and in the next hot second, our lips press together.

This is no butterfly kiss.

No earlobe nibble.

It's full-on. No holds barred.

The waves lap lazily on the shore as our lips crash together, a hungry, needy kiss.

I should stop. Really, I should.

But fuck stopping.

This will have to be our last kiss, so I'm making the best of it.

I take charge, caressing her cheek, sliding my thumb along her jaw.

Deepening the kiss even more.

My tongue slides between her lips, and she parts for me, and this is all there is. The waiters, the couples, the beach itself all slip out of focus as my world narrows to only her.

The taste of her lips.

The feel of her kiss.

The soft little sigh she makes as we slow things down.

Then a sweet, almost shy murmur.

Which is funny because London doesn't seem shy.

Except sometimes she does.

This woman is full of contradictions and complexities, and I want to explore them.

I want to uncover them with her, be the one to learn everything she likes, and then give that to her, do that to her, for her.

Except I can't.

I have to remember that.

That was one last kiss.

She sinks back in her chair, and I do the same, and we look at each other like *What's next?*

But what's next is work.

I need to stay the course. I'm about to tell her there are rules, since she might not know, but she speaks first, exhaling deeply, like she's both relieved and delighted.

"Thank you for saying yes. My brother is going to be so thrilled."

I blink, trying to connect the dots between the work project and her brother.

"Why would he be excited?"

Another grin comes my way. "He runs the club."

The ultimate record scratch rends the air, and the whole place goes silent.

I'm imagining things. She can't possibly have said that.

Not the guy who signs my checks. Not the guy I genuinely look up to. Not the guy who's awesome to work for.

I must have heard her wrong. "He runs the club?" I ask, in a voice that barely sounds like my own.

"Archer. He's my brother. You probably know him."

I drop my head in my hands as all my luck drains away.

6

Fact one: I just had the best first date of my life.

Fact two: I want to kiss her again and again, and pretty much do everything else with her that you do without clothes.

Fact three: She seems to want the same things I do.

Fact four: She's London Hollis. My boss's little sister.

That final fact obviates everything that precedes it. Doesn't matter how true facts one to three are. Nothing can come of them.

I've been there. I've done that.

I'm not getting on that merry-go-round again.

That's where things got messy with Tracy.

Or messier, I should say. I worked for her father, and we were all kinds of connected.

Tracy and I met at a Decemberists show at the Roxy and started dating quickly. Turned out our mutual love of music was more than a hobby, and she introduced me to her dad, the president of Loud Nation, the largest collective of radio stations on the West Coast. He pulled some strings and got me a plum gig hosting my own show. Sure, that show was on-air at four in the morning, but it was still mine, a dream come true. In that satellite studio in Hollywood, DJ Insomnia was born. I was building a name for myself, ascending the ranks way faster than I could have on my own.

But when everything went belly-up with Tracy, so did the job with Loud Nation. Tracy pulled the rug out from under our relationship, and the whole house of vinyl came tumbling down. Her father terminated my show, and effectively barred me from doing anything else with Loud Nation. End of side A, please flip the record over.

Like I was the one who needed to be taught a lesson.

But I learned it the hard way. And now I live it, abiding by my own rules regardless of what company policy dictates. *Don't mix work and dating.* Don't date coworkers, clients, or business partners. Don't take out the boss's daughter, the boss's sister, or the boss's second cousin.

I'm not interested in taking those risks again. I'd be a fool.

This time, I'm doing things on my own. I'm making good money and having a great time working at the club. I've got my weekly show on-air with the local public radio station. The pay isn't great, but I have more control over the music I play, and the time slot is better. I have to stay focused—I've worked too hard to get back to this spot post-Tracy.

I can't chance sliding to the starting block again, especially when there's a raise on the line. I want that raise. Just as soon as I hit the one-year mark next month.

After I pay the check and walk London to her car, I inhale the salty ocean air and then I level with her. We've been honest all along. No reason to stop now.

"Look, I would love nothing more than to see you again and take you out again and kiss you again. And I'm just going to be totally blunt—I want to take you home."

She lowers her face and presses her fingers against the bridge of her nose, right under her glasses. "I want all that too, and I feel like such an idiot."

My heart lurches toward her. I *want* to reassure her.

But I can't. If I don't say this, I will push her up against the car, pull those glasses off her face, and kiss her under the moon until we both see stars.

"But there are club rules," I say. "No messing around with employees, and even if those rules didn't exist, you're my boss's sister." It sounds like a joke when it comes out of my mouth, like karma is fucking with me, and I honestly don't know what I've done to piss off the cosmic gods.

Her brown eyes lock with mine, and she lifts her arm like she's going to squeeze mine or grab my wrist. But she must think better of it because she drops her hand back to her side. "No, Teddy. I didn't mean to put you in a bad place. I should have thought of that—my brother and the club rules and all. But I met you and we had a connection, and I guess I thought . . ." She slows down, meets my eyes again with that fire in hers, and in a softer voice says, "We had such an intense spark that I honestly wasn't thinking about rules. The whole time at dinner, I was in the moment, having a good time. A great time."

I reach my hand behind my neck and squeeze. Tension radiates through my body. I need to find a way to release this energy other than slamming my mouth to hers because that is one of the coolest things a woman has ever said to me—that she was so caught up in the energy, the chemistry, that she wasn't thinking about games or rules or how things are supposed to be, or if you call someone after the first date or not. Things I'm honestly not sure about either, but would want to figure out with her.

But here we are, cutting it off already. "Listen, tonight was great. I'm pretty sure it's going to go down in a hall of records somewhere as the best first date ever."

She smiles, soft and warm and so genuine. "It definitely is. There's no way anybody anywhere ever had a better first date than us."

I try not to grin like a fool. But it's impossible when she says stuff like that. "Let's just be honest. We set the bar tonight. This was the best first date in the history of time."

"It absolutely was. People will be talking about it for ages," she says, her smile making my heart flip.

Which isn't helpful.

Not one bit.

"But, listen, my last relationship was all tangled up with work and family stuff. I need this job," I say. "And I can't. I just can't."

She holds up a hand, her voice so understanding. "You don't have to justify anything to me. I totally get it. We're on the same page. We are 100 percent on the same page, and I'm sorry I didn't think about it before. I should have. I really should have." She flicks me a flirty look, like she's so damn good at. "But you're kind of adorable."

"Adorable?"

"Adorable is a good thing. Do not question the adorable compliment. It's up there with hot, sexy, and smoking, but kind of better. In a class by itself."

Here I thought adorable was reserved for puppies and grandmas. But nope, turns out adorable is hot. London thinks I'm hot.

I want to ride the high of that compliment.

Only, it doesn't matter, since I need to stay focused on the reality of the situation.

I steer us toward safer waters. "Maybe we should just work together on this project of yours. I would love to help you. It would bring me a lot of pleasure," I say, trying to tread carefully around that land mine of a word.

"So we'll be friends," she says in invitation, like it's the most wonderful thing in the world, the idea of us becoming friends.

Maybe it is. Maybe becoming friends could be fantastic.

Except . . .

Even I'm not so much of an optimist or a fool that I believe that. You don't kiss someone the way we kissed and then make each other friendship bracelets.

But you don't kiss someone the way we kissed, learn she's your boss's sister, and keep moving forward either.

So, this is it.

We trade phone numbers.

For work, rather than for *us*.

When I open the door of her cherry-red VW bug, we lock eyes and hesitate. I don't think either one of us is ready to say goodbye.

"I really did have an incredible time tonight," she says as she slides into her seat. Somehow I find the will to resist bending down and kissing her one more time. Kissing her ear the way she likes it. Brushing my lips against hers, drawing out one or more of her sexy little sighs.

I'm not kidding when I say it's one of the hardest things I've ever had to do.

* * *

I trudge up the steps to my condo, unlock the door, and am greeted by fifty pounds of *I don't care if you just had the worst best-date-ever, it's time to show me all your affection*.

David Bowie licks my face and gives that happy whine that says no matter how badly that sucker punch of a date hurts, he's still happy to see me.

Which is reason number 10,522 why I love this dog.

I scratch his head. "Hey there, bud."

I leash him up and pop next door to Mrs. Morales's place.

It's ten o'clock, but the lights are on. That's my sign that it's okay to knock.

Sherri opens the door, beaming up at me. "*Mira.* One of my favorite neighbors."

I sigh in mock indignation. "I can't believe I have to compete with Sam for that honor. Is Vin Scully *listo?*"

Her little beagle, named after the greatest sports broadcaster of all time, answers the question of whether he's ready by jumping on my leg.

She clips on his blue leash, which matches his adorable Dodgers bandana. "*Tú eres un ángel, oso de peluche.*"

I smile at Sherri's term of endearment. She has called me Teddy Bear ever since I moved across from her. Growing up in Los Angeles, I learned to speak Spanish from an early age, so Sherri and I switch back and forth between languages when we talk, like we're playing verbal hopscotch. "Ah, now you're pretending I am your favorite."

"*Absolutamente.* Since you're taking him for his late-night escapades."

"*Por nada.*" That's the truth. I walk her guy with mine nearly every night—if I'm home before midnight.

She gives me a curious once-over, eyeing my jeans and crisp white linen shirt, sleeves rolled halfway up my forearms. "You're looking sharp." She winks. "Did you swipe right on someone? I bet she swiped right back." She taps her chin. "Wait. Is that how it works? It's right when you like someone? Left when you just want a hookup?" She lowers her voice to a whisper. "Did you have a hookup tonight?"

I laugh. "It's swipe right. You just swipe right."

"Ah, so you like her?"

"What? Where did you get that from? I just said swipe right."

She gives me a motherly smirk. "But you said more . . . *con tus ojos*," she adds, waving her fingers over her eyes. "Do we need to crack open some beers and chat all about your new woman?"

New woman. Do I ever like the sound of that.

But it's not meant to be with London.

"I did have a date," I say with a wistful sigh, "but we can't call her my new woman."

Sherri taps her wrist, indicating the time. Then she arches a questioning brow. "It's just after ten, and you're in your date clothes, showing off your tattoo," she says, waving to my forearm where a hint of ink edges out beneath my sleeve. "Yet you're taking the dogs out. Either it's going to be a late-night date, or you're home earlier than you'd like. Jansen hasn't even finished getting this save yet," she says as the Dodgers' game plays from a radio.

Sighing, I flash back on London's words from earlier. "It's complicated."

"Then maybe you do need that beer."

Bowie paws at me, and Vin Scully whimpers. "Maybe I do. But for now, I'll take the guys for a walk. And let me know when you want Sam and me to come over and move that couch for you. That is, if you still need that from your favorite neighbor—me—and your second favorite—him."

"Anytime this week would be great from my

favorites. Or," she says, raising a finger, like she just thought of something, "maybe when Sam is leaving for work. *No es una mala idea.*"

"I get you, *abuela* Sherri." I drop my voice to a whisper. "But he doesn't wear the costumes *to* work. He puts them on *at* work."

"At. On. In. Off. It all works for me." She waves a hand airily.

I give her a tip of the figurative cap. "We'll pop in at some point, and I'll make sure Sam is wearing a shirt this time."

"You'll do nothing of the sort."

"I know. Just messing with you," I say as I head off with the pooches, hoping the walk will take my mind off London.

As if it could.

* * *

After I drop Vin Scully following our tour, Bowie and I head into my home. I flop on my bed, my chest heavy, and I give myself a pep talk.

Shake it off. She's just a woman. It was only one date. It's nothing to be disappointed about. It happens. It's like when you miss a turn on your GPS and go a mile or two out of your way—annoying, but you get over it.

This date-turned-not-date is a minor hiccup in my day. Even so, I turn to my best friend and say, "What am I going to do?"

Bowie spies his favorite stuffed monkey on the bed, mounts it, and gives it a few pumps.

I roll my eyes. "No. Not that. Trust me, I wish."

He stops and licks my face, and I laugh. "Did that. Wish I could do that again too."

But I can't. No matter how much I want to, I simply cannot.

I roll over in bed and turn off the light. Tonight is an early one for DJ Insomnia.

7

That night

From the Woman Power Trio, aka the text messages of London and her two besties, Olive and Emery

London: What is that saying about modern dating?

Olive: The scary thing about dating is you're either going to marry the person or break up?

Emery: OMG, DID YOU GET MARRIED TONIGHT? YOU'RE IN TROUBLE FOR NOT INVITING US, LONDON.

Olive: Big trouble. Like I-will-never-loan-you-those-black-patent-leather-heels-I-got-from-Target-that-you-love-and-they-don't-make-anymore trouble.

London: One, you will never stop loaning me those shoes. They're like our *Sisterhood of the Traveling Pants* shoes. And two, the saying is more like dating and Murphy's Law.

Olive: Oh. Well, my second choice was going to be "Dating is like the tenth circle of hell." That's another saying.

Emery: Says the woman who is happily married to a guy who walked into her bar two years ago.

Olive: It happens! I got lucky. Anyway, what's the problem, London? You learned the guy you like doesn't do his own laundry? Is he your first cousin? Or does he believe we are all here as part of an alien plot to take over Earth? Was there no spark?

London: There was so much spark!

Emery: The problem is alien, then?

London: Worse. He's a genuinely nice guy. He says we can't date because he works for my brother, and because I'm technically an Edge employee too right now. And—cue heavy sighs—he's right. Plus, his last relationship was tangled up with his work. And, of course, him actually being, ya know, thoughtful and principled makes me like him even more.

Emery: Ah, so he is an alien—a good guy.

London: Yes. He's an alien, Emery. I dated an alien. And I kissed an alien too.

Olive: Ooh, I just finished this super-hot book about a double-dicked alien who gives quadruple orgasms to Earth ladies. That's what he calls them—Earth ladies. And trust me, in Dax Long's voice, nothing sounds hotter. But enough about twin dicks. My condolences on your date . . . not being a dick.

Emery: How dare he be considerate?

London: Tell me about it. But hey, Teddy and I will be friends. It'll be great. I'll keep the laser focus on work and friendship, friendship and work. Besides, that's what I should be focused on now that I'm back in town regardless.

Olive: I agree. You need to nail that opportunity you've been telling us about.

London: And nail it I will! I'll be all work, work, work, friends, friends, friends with Teddy.

Emery: Have fun being friends with a guy you want to bang, bang, bang, no matter how many alien dicks he has.

Olive: He has two, Em. Two.

Emery: I'd have thought he has three, what with all that spark.

8

The next morning, the sun blares through my window, the coffee machine whirrs, and I put on my game face. It's Monday, so the club is closed, giving me a chance to work on my business plan. Edge is fun, but I'm pretty sure deejaying a part-time all-male revue has a shelf life. And though my weekly radio show is a blast, my dreams are bigger. That's why during my free time I pour my energy into building up DJ Insomnia's full-service event business, All Night Entertainment.

The website is up and running, all the social media platforms are covered, and I've invested in a great road kit and some killer lights to bring the party wherever I go. Now, I need clients.

That's all.

I roll up my sleeves, so to speak, and do my damnedest to find them.

I spend some time cold-contacting various community organizations in town: churches, temples, rec centers. I fire off tons of emails, crack my knuckles, stretch, and feel pretty good about my progress so far today.

Better, in fact, when my inbox displays one new message right away. This is awesome. I bet a church has already responded with *Yes. And can I please book you for this weekend's potluck?*

But when I click over to the email, my heart sinks a little bit.

Or maybe it's not my heart. What's the organ in your body that hosts all of the guilt that you feel? Oh, it's pretty much your entire bloodstream, and mine is coursing with a whole lot of guilt right now thanks to an email from the boss.

I click it open, a bit of regret swirling around in my chest as I read Archer's message.

Hey, Teddy, just a quick note to let you know that double bachelorette party on Thursday just became a TRIPLE. I don't think we've ever done a triple bachelorette party before! But I am up to the challenge. Hoping you can get to work a half hour early to make sure everything is a go with the music?

I reply instantly.

Absolutely. I'll be there, and I'll tweak my set list to add even more awesomeness. It's going to be a fantastic night!

. . .

I add an exclamation point at the end. I'm not an exclamation point kind of guy, but I'm going to sell this with all the exclamation points in the world. I hit send. As the message flies off into cyberspace, I choose to see his email as a reminder.

A reminder that I cannot pass Go again. I'm playing Monopoly, and I'm putting myself in jail for the rest of the game.

I click over to my texts and look up London's name, then I fire off a professional note.

That's all it is.

Just a text about working on her project.

Nothing more.

Teddy: Hey! When do you want to get together to talk music and dancing? I have time this afternoon or tomorrow. What's good for you?

I read it over.

Yup.

There's nothing flirty. Nothing dirty.

I hit send, then it's time for a midmorning tennis session with Sam. I pull on workout shorts and a stretchy polo, walk Bowie around the block, then pop down the hall and grab Sam to take off for the public courts at Vermont Canyon.

* * *

An hour later we're both drenched in sweat, my heart rate is up somewhere between "power walk" and "chased by wolves," and I'm ready to put the nail in the coffin of this match. Sam might have the looks of an athlete, but hand-eye coordination seems to have eluded him.

Lucky for me.

I finish him off with a powerful forehand down the line, which he misses by a mile.

Sam rips his headband off, his blond hair flying around his face. "Damn you, Teddy," he screams like he's McEnroe. His yell morphs into a laugh as he calls, "Good game," while retrieving the ball.

"It's always a good game when I win," I say as we head toward the bench at the side of the court to grab our gear.

"You can't bait me. I don't feel bad over losing. Not wired that way. I feel good even when you destroy me," Sam says with a *just try me* grin. Pretty sure he was born meditating. The dude defines chill.

"Perks of playing with you. I've never met anyone who seems to enjoy losing as much as you do," I say as I twist the top off my water bottle.

"Life is infinite, and everything is meaningless. The journey is all that matters, not the score." Sam lifts his face to the sky like he's inhaling good vibes from the sun. "And you were going extra hard out there today, my friend. Seemed liked you were trying to hit more than just the ball," he says, lifting a brow in a silent question.

I know what he's asking—*how did the date go?*

I told him about it on the way to sushi last night. Well, I told him that I was going out with someone I'd just met.

Right as I'm about to deflect my friend's astute observations, my phone pings. I check the text immediately, my pulse spiking when I see London's name.

Great. Fucking great. My body's reaction to her replying to my text isn't going to make this easy.

London: Happy Monday! Are you a Monday person? Confession: I am. Mondays get a bad rap, but I think they're a great chance to do ALL THE THINGS. Today is great for a brainstorm sesh. I can't thank you enough for helping me.

Teddy: I'm afraid I've got to side with Garfield on Mondays. No use for 'em. That said, since you're all up in Monday's business, I'm willing to give it a shot. Where do you want to meet?

London: Perfect. Meet at McConnell's Ice Cream in Grand Central Market at two? Maybe I can change your mind about Mondays.

I whip off a quick reply and tell her I'll see her soon. When I look up, I meet a set of curious eyes, asking what the fuck I am up to.

"And who might that be that you responded to so

quickly, you eager beaver?" Sam tosses his towel over his shoulders as we make our way off the court.

"London. The woman I went out with last night."

"Next-day text from her. Nice. Things must have gone well," he says with an arm punch as we walk to the parking lot.

"They went great. Better than great. It was an awesome date, man. We both have dogs, we're both into music, we laughed a ton, and we can talk about pretty much anything, it seems."

"Sounds like you're building to an epic *but* here, man."

My shoulders sag. "But . . . she's Archer's little sister."

He stops in his tracks. Blinks. Stares, like I can't have said that. "Archer, like the boss man Archer? Archer, who runs the club?"

"That Archer."

He winces, with a sad look that says *Sucks to be you.* "Dude. That's *no bueno, man.* I didn't even know Archer had a sister."

"He does. And she's awesome. And gorgeous. And—"

"Totally off-limits," Sam cuts me off before I can finish. He's not wrong.

I was hoping the bright light of day would help me see this situation from a new angle, but all roads still point to not-going-to-happen. "Yes, she's off-limits," I repeat as we resume our pace. I say it once more in my head—the reminder is helpful.

Necessary too.

"How did you leave things with her? You didn't fuck, did you?"

I pause long enough to think about how incredible she must be in bed. Her body is killer, her wit lightning sharp. And with our chemistry, I'm certain the sex between us would be electric. Giving and taking, taking and giving. Learning what she likes. Doing that *to* her, *for* her . . . But I'll never find out.

"We didn't sleep together. We kissed, and it was incredible. Then she mentioned who her brother was and that she's here doing work for the club. And pretty much all hope of a future date shriveled up and died then."

He brings his hand to his heart. "I mourn the shriveling of your hope, bro."

"Thanks. Appreciate it."

"And then, I presume, you were all enlightened and wise, agreed to go your separate ways, and wished each other the best?"

We reach my car as I turn over what he said—which is *not* at all what London and I did last night. "Actually, we were enlightened, as you say, in another way. We agreed to put our feelings aside and focus on working together." As those words come out, they sound . . . *too wise*. "I'm meeting her this afternoon to help with some new choreography for her show."

A laugh bursts from him as he draws air quotes. "'Help with some new choreography'?"

"Yes. That's what I said."

He holds up a hand and forces himself to stop laughing. "Sounds like a euphemism."

I furrow my brow. "It's not a euphemism for sex. We are legit meeting for work stuff."

He shakes his head. "No, man. Sounds like a euphemism for how painful your lack of a love life is about to become."

"Thanks. Thanks a lot."

"Don't shoot the messenger. You're the guy who just signed up to help a babe you like with"—he stops to chuckle—"*choreography*."

And he's right. Helping her with dance moves sounds like a recipe for disaster. Too bad I left my earthquake kit at home.

I load the rackets into the trunk of my car.

"You have time to swing by Ricky's? Grab some fish tacos?" Sam asks.

I look him dead in the eye and tell him a universal truth. "I always have time for fish tacos."

Tacos for lunch, ice cream for a snack, and my radio show tonight? Plus, some London time? Mondays might be looking up after all.

9

Monday afternoon

From the Woman Power Trio, aka the text messages of London and her two besties, Olive and Emery

London: LADIES.

Olive: Uh-oh. She's breaking out the all caps.

Emery: That means shit just got serious. London is about to take a pledge.

London: THE ALL CAPS PLEDGE.

Olive: I am listening.

London: I CAN PULL OFF THIS WHOLE WORK-AND-FRIENDSHIP THING WITH TEDDY. WATCH ME. I DID MY YOGA. I SET MY INTENTION FOR THE DAY.

Olive: And that intention is to refrain from jumping on the guy you're hot for?

London: Yes. My intention is work-related. Not spark-related.

Olive: Or three-dick-related. You're not touching any of his three alien dicks?

London: THERE WILL BE NO DICKING, ALIEN OR OTHERWISE.

Emery: Impressive restraint. Yoga is indeed good to you.

London: When I see him, I'm going to discuss my routine and ask questions. Like what kind of music works with this routine? What genres play well in the club? What inspires you creatively?

Olive: "Seeing your ankles over my shoulders inspires me." (BTW, I totes said that in a deep, sexy, manly voice.)

Emery: We know!

London: Your man-voice is so sexy, Liv. Also, ankles-over-shoulders-related-questions are off-limits. Along with another question I won't ask: if I wasn't your boss's little sister, would you press your body against mine and kiss me until my lips were bruised, my knees wobbled, and my stomach flipped?

Olive: Pro tip? Also don't ask, "Do you want to go home with me so I can show you how flexible I am?"

Emery: She is super flexible. It's pretty impressive.

London: *sends selfie of touching my elbow with my tongue*

Olive: Stahp, stahp. You're turning me on, and I need to go make drinks.

Emery: I need to get back to work. I have pitch meetings, and now all I can think about is London's elbow tongue twisters, you pervert!

London: Are you impressed with how I got all my pervy tendencies out with you two clowns?

Emery: Yes, but if he's into elbow licking, we have other issues.

Olive: Issues I want to hear about! I love kinks. Any kinks, even elbow-licking ones.

London: There will be no elbow licking or other displays of flexibility.

Emery: But if you do cave, send a full report.

London: I WILL NOT CAVE. YOU HAVE MY WORD.

10

I pop out of the Pershing Square subway station shortly before two with my most comfortable Chucks on my feet and one gorgeous brunette on my mind. I'm not entirely sure what London has planned for this brainstorming session, but the fact that I'm going to see her again works for me.

Except that is the kind of dangerous thinking I need to avoid. London is off-limits. *Period.* It's a damn good thing she set this meetup at one of LA's busiest locations. A public spot to talk over some ice cream guarantees we won't make out like teenagers an hour before curfew.

As I enter the bustling market, the smells of barbecue, pupusas, and fresh-baked bread assault my senses in the best way. Some parts of LA can make you feel like you're traveling the world without leaving the city, and Grand Central Market is like that, with its eclectic mix of international cuisine. From homemade pastas to grandma's tamales, this place has whatever I'm craving.

As I turn down an aisle, the McConnell's Ice Cream sign beckons, as does the woman standing under it. My gaze locks onto a pair of red glasses framing deep brown eyes that I swear, even with yards of space and dozens of people between us, are looking at me like she's as psyched for our second date as I am.

Nope. Stop. This is not a date.

This is definitely not our second date.

It's our third.

The dog park was kind of the first. Sushi was the second. So, if it were a date, which it is not, this would be number three.

I need to slam the brakes on that kind of thinking. Trouble is, slowing this car keeps getting harder because none of my thoughts about London are friendly.

Very few are professional.

I take in her loosely braided hair and the way those jeans were made for her curves.

As I make my way to her, I smile and offer her a one-armed hug, because this thing between us needs to stay aboveboard. I value my job, I respect her brother, and I don't want a repeat of what happened with Tracy's dad. I have to keep my personal life and my professional life in their own lanes, double yellow line between them.

Better yet, a retaining wall.

But the scent of orange peel takes over and derails my train of thought.

I linger in the hug for longer than I should.

When we break apart, I try to clear my head and control my pulse. Work meetings should not get my heart rate up to wind-sprints level. "Great to see you again. But ice cream before dinner? You are trying to make me enjoy Monday, aren't you?"

"That's the goal. I intend to change your mind about Mondays." Her smile curves slightly higher on one side of her mouth, and I'll be damned if it's not the cutest thing ever. "I hope this place works for you."

"Absolutely. I love the market. I even took the train down from my place. Super easy."

She shoots me an *I'm impressed* look. "I didn't think anybody took public transportation in LA."

"I'm not sure anybody does, but hey, they built it—may as well give it a shot. Plus, let's be honest—driving is the worst."

"Driving is almost as painful as finding out the adorable guy you want to date is off-limits," she says.

I laugh. "Still not as painful as finding out the adorable woman you want to date is off-limits. That's the worst of the worst."

I'm glad we've got that out in the open.

That we're acknowledging the score.

And that we're going to stick to the plan.

If she can be up-front about this, I can too.

Hell, we've *got* this.

Cutting through the din of the open-air market, Ben Folds's "The Luckiest" blares from a boom box on a nearby deli counter. London points toward the music. "But hearing this song? Definitely not the worst. This song rocks."

"Best of the best. Ben Folds is a stellar songwriter."

I have a theory about certain songs. Sometimes

something happens in your life and a song you've heard a thousand times becomes new again. You hear it as though for the first time, because in many ways it is.

This could be one of those moments—an old song becoming new.

But that seems like an observation you might share with someone on a date—not at a business meeting between two like-minded professionals who are putting their careers first. Maybe there'll be another time for it.

For now, it's time for ice cream. "Want to grab those cones?" I ask.

"It's like you can read my mind. Shall we walk and talk? I do my best thinking on my feet, especially when powered by my favorite food group."

"Walk and talk and eat is a great idea. McConnell's has the best mint chip in the city, so I'm an easy date. Plus, I've been told that counts as a veggie."

"You're learning my ice cream ways," she teases.

"I find ice cream logic quite convincing."

We step up to the refrigerated countertop to order. While my heart may be set on mint chip, the swirls of strawberries and cream and gooey chunks of white-chocolate raspberry are too tempting to resist.

I avail myself of the generous sampling policy, trying both.

London rolls her eyes. "You are powerless to resist the sample."

"No one can resist. Plus, it's fruit and veggie and dairy and everything my body needs." I could say the same about London—my body needs this gorgeous woman, and God, I'd like to sample more of her.

She holds up her hands, shaking her head. "No need to justify the science of ice cream to me, nor the philosophy of free samples."

I opt for mint chip in a waffle cone, and London picks a cup of salted caramel with graham crackers, claiming it meets the daily quota for grains. My wallet is out and ready to go, but she sets a hand on my arm, and my brain melts faster than this double scoop. "My invite, my treat," she says as she swipes her card.

I like to treat a woman when we go out, but this isn't a date and it's not my place to push. Plus, I'm not gonna lie—it's pretty sexy to see her being both considerate and assertive at the same time.

Not that her sexiness matters. This isn't our second date, or our third date, and we already outlined the off-limits rules mere minutes ago.

Once we're a safe distance away from the shop, London shoots me a playful look. "You said at the get-go that you wanted mint chip."

I take a slow lick from my cone. "I did say that. But I can *think* I know what I want and not be sure until I've done some taste-testing. Experimentation is the key to self-awareness."

"Props for the application of the scientific method, but it sounds like you're an ice cream rake."

My brow knits. "What's an ice cream *rake*?"

"Like a Victorian-era man who enjoys all the ladies. All the flavors. Like Willoughby from *Sense and Sensibility* or Wickham from the best book ever."

"That's me. I'm an ice cream rake, like those two." I chuckle and shake my head. "No, I'm more of a Wentworth-style one-shop man. Once you've picked the right parlor, though, it's fun to explore the menu."

With a look of contentment, she crooks a smile, then says, "Happiness is all about exploring ice cream flavors."

"I can't argue with that." As I lick the mint chip, I wiggle my fingers on my free hand, the sign for her to tell me everything. "All right. Lay it on me. I want to know the details of this epic new dance show you've planned."

She spreads her arms wide, practically bouncing as we walk. "This is my plan. Everyone knows *Magic Mike*, right?"

I scoff. "Of course. *Magic Mike* is a cultural institution, along the lines of Michelangelo and Shakespeare."

She raises a *you don't say* eyebrow. "Oh, absolutely. *Magic Mike*'s legacy is secure for the rest of time, right alongside other titans like Jane Austen and Charlotte Brontë."

I smile at her. "London, did you bring up Jane Austen so that I would ask about Mr. Darcy?"

She brings her hand to her chest in a *What? Not me* gesture. "Actually, I'm a little offended that you haven't asked about him yet."

"You know what? I'm kind of offended at myself too. What is wrong with me?" I clear my throat and place my hand over my heart in exaggerated shame. "How is Mr. Darcy, and do you have any pictures of him today?"

"Maybe," she says coyly, and whips out her phone. She scrolls through a copious amount of sunbathing pooch poses.

"He could be a dog model."

She slugs my arm playfully. "Thank you. Also, nice save making up for forgetting to ask about him."

"Whew. Okay. He's a stunner," I add as she tucks the phone into her purse. "But back to *Magic Mike*. Cultural institution, right up there with Rembrandt and Vonnegut. And honestly? It's kind of a good movie," I say as we round the corner.

"Shockingly good, and not just because my friends and I wanted to throw dollar bills at the screen," she says, almost like a whispered confession, before continuing. "So, for the routine, I'm envisioning this: *Magic Mike*, but instead of the oiled-up, half-naked men, we have tastefully clothed, confident women. Instead of the hip-grinding gyrations, it's more effortless fluidity. And in place of that brutish sexuality, we have more nuanced, playful sensuality."

"Okay." I draw out the word out as I track her train of thought, or try to. "So, nothing like *Magic Mike*."

"Except . . . good dancing," she points out.

"True. Gotta give Channing and the crew props for those moves. I sort of hate to admit it, but I've seen the movie a couple of times."

She nudges me with her elbow. "Look at you, Mr. *Magic Mike* fan."

I raise my hands in surrender, one of them still holding the cone. "Look, I . . ." I'm about to say my ex loved the movie and insisted on watching it. But I don't feel like talking about Tracy, so I let the sentence die.

But somehow London reads into my silence, and

softly, in a kind voice, she says, "Let me guess. You had an ex who liked the movie?"

"Yes." I sigh, but I'm relieved that she figured it out quickly. That I don't have to be the one to bring up the ex. "I was involved with someone for a long time. She actually really loved the flick and wanted to watch it a lot."

London shakes her spoon in my face. "We've cracked this open. We're going to have the ex conversation," she says, and she's so open about career, life, love, and *un-love*. That's a refreshing change from the norm.

Plus, I'm the guy I am now partly because of all the shit that went wrong with Tracy. The problems we had helped me see what I don't want and what I do. "I went out with this woman for about three years. It ended badly, as things with exes sometimes do. She cheated on me with the dog walker."

I say it clinically, not wanting to give this too much weight. Tracy doesn't deserve the air space. "Everything was tangled up, though, because I worked for her father. That's one of the main reasons I'm trying to be careful about getting involved with anyone who's close to my job."

London shoots me a smile, a soft, sympathetic one. But it's not an *I feel sorry for you* smile—more like an *I get it, and you were dealt a shitty hand* smile. I appreciate the difference—that *she* sees the difference.

"That sucks. I'm sorry you went through that. It's terrible when people lie to each other and deceive each other. So what if she liked the dog walker? She should have just left to be with him."

Yes! I want to shout it, exclamation point and all.

"Exactly! Sure, I cared about her and I loved her, but if she was done with the relationship, she could have just left it. Don't cheat. Get out of it and live your life, and don't be a liar. And don't make a liar out of me and the life we had together," I say.

London spoons another bite of ice cream and nods several times. "I completely agree. My situation isn't exactly like that, but I dated someone in college, and we stayed together much longer than we should have. I think we were both afraid to end it, and we expended a lot of energy to try to make it work. And it didn't. He was a great guy, and I really liked him, but we didn't have that spark. That was a while ago though. I've been single for a long time."

Her reflection on past relationships makes me think she'd be a considerate girlfriend, and that . . . that sounds terrific.

For someone else.

Not for me.

"Spark is pretty damn important," I say, keeping my response broad. "Spark is definitely powerful, and it matters."

Her eyes gleam with excitement and maybe under-standing as they lock with mine while we walk. "It does. Spark is real. We have to listen to the spark. Well, some-times," she adds under her breath.

Perhaps that's her reminder that we can't act on this electricity between us.

My mind latches on to a comment she made last

night. "Is he the reason you said things were compli-cated in Vegas?"

"Yes. He's exactly why I said that. He moved there with me, and it didn't work out. When we ended things, I started putting me first. Been married to my career ever since."

Which raises an interesting point—one I'm damn curious about. "What's the endgame for you? You know it's not deejaying at a part-time all-male revue for me—what is it for you?"

We cross another block, and it's hard to walk and watch her smile with anticipation and pride. "There's this really fantastic producer that I want to work with, André Davies. I was telling my girlfriends about him the other night. He travels a ton, but he's based out of LA. He's incredibly innovative and cutting edge, with thought-provoking music videos plus these flash-mob-type TikTok videos. They're so unexpected, and the dancing always looks familiar but new somehow." Her voice is absolutely musical with excitement as she tells me more. "I'm assembling a portfolio of clips I'm calling *The Unexpected*. Hopefully once he sees it, he'll know he needs to have someone with my vision on his team."

"Well, then," I say, finishing my cone as she tosses her cup and spoon into a recycling can. "Let's create the unexpected."

"And that starts with the music. Though, if it were entirely up to me, my life would be told to a soundtrack of Sam Smith," she says, dipping her chin like she's admitted something secret.

"Nothing wrong with Sam Smith. That dude is a

seriously soulful crooner. But his songs are more like the soundtrack of those TV shows where people are constantly breaking up."

A laugh bursts from her, and I love that sound, love how easily it comes. "True. But I like to dance to him, so he works for me. Who do you want to craft your background music?"

"I'm taking the deejay exemption. I won't play favorites. I need *all the music* to soundtrack my life."

"So greedy."

"I'm musically gluttonous, and I'm owning it."

"Very clever, pulling that deejay exemption card. You've got a lot going on in that pretty head of yours." She playfully musses my hair, and goose bumps jump down my spine. Did she just call me pretty? I'm into that, but it's best not to let on how much, so I get back to why we're hanging out today. "So, are you going to use the dance you choreograph for Edge as an in with this Davies guy?"

"Yes. That's the plan. I'll shoot a video of the routine so I can include it with my portfolio. Shay Sloan, the woman I worked with in Vegas, is also keeping her eye open for opportunities for me, so I'll send the video to her too. I need to find that perfect combination of my moves set to the right beat that gives that playful, fun, out-on-the-town vibe with a touch of the iconic. Millennial chic meets hipster fleek."

"Do people still say 'fleek'? I don't think that's a thing anymore," I chide. Despite the jokes, this conversation underlines that going to Monopoly jail doesn't protect only my career aspirations. London has goals too that extend beyond the club. They tap into her natural creativity, and I want to be able to help her.

There's more at stake here than whether I want a third or fourth date with her, than whether I want to take her home, strip her down to nothing, and kiss her all over. Than whether I want to learn if she likes it when I lick the hollow of her throat, the valley of her breasts, her belly, and if she likes to be undressed slowly or quickly, and . . . FUUUUCKK.

I am getting off topic right now.

"I can give you some suggestions or play some tracks for you," I say, reorienting my thoughts as best I can. "But it might help if I saw these moves in action. To give me a better sense of what you're going for."

Might give me a better sense of how sexy she is too, but I don't say that out loud.

A wicked glint flashes in her eyes. "Follow me." She wiggles her fingers. She jogs halfway down the block, points to a door, punches a combo on a keypad, then disappears into the entrance of the Theatre at Ace Hotel, a former movie house that's been renovated into a live performance venue.

When I catch up, she's holding the door open for me, and naturally, I have no choice but to follow her.

11

I'm damn curious how she finagled her way into this theater. "Hey, magician. How did you just walk into the Ace like that?"

"I know the house manager," she says, looking all manic-pixie-dream-girl for a hot second. "Texted him earlier. He told me we could have the stage to ourselves for an hour. It's all ours."

She runs through the ornate lobby, then past a set of double doors that lead down the aisle past the seats. When she reaches the stage, she hops up onto it, tucks her glasses into her purse, and drops it on the side of the stage. I trail behind, taking in the grandeur of the empty Gothic theater.

My eyes eventually land on London where she stands, hands on hips, right in the middle of the stage.

I take a seat in the front row, and this is definitely the best front-row seat I've ever had. The stage is washed in a soft blue light, and London sets up the routine. "I imagine this is a synchronized set with maybe four or five women. They sashay to center stage as the lights come up and the amazing music that you're going to help me choose begins. Hold for four." London freezes, reminding me of a statue of Aphrodite. "Then five, six, seven, eight . . ."

She slides into that classic stripper move where she drops her head, jams both hands into her hair, flips her head back, and pumps out her hips.

That move works fantastically well on London's body—and on mine, judging from the wood I'm now sporting.

Thanks, dick. Really fucking helpful.

With a snap of her hips, the energy of the dance shifts. It's raw, sexy, with familiar moves, like the sway of her body and the slide of her hands traveling down between her breasts.

As the choreography teeters on the brink of red-hot sexuality, her movements morph into something fun and playful, like at any moment she might raise her hands, whoop, and holler, which is exactly what the crowd wants to do sometimes.

A few beats later, the dance turns quieter, softer, more sensual, more erotic.

I am transfixed. I can't look away. She's done everything she said she would do. She's created something completely unexpected.

The creative part of my brain is offering an encouraging *yes*.

The dirty part of my brain is shouting, *Holy hell, get over here. Get off the stage and get on top of me and ride me so fucking hard in the middle of this theater.*

And the rational, logical part of my brain agrees, saying, *Well, that would be an excellent idea, and you should absolutely do that.*

Then there's that voice, the dude-bro in me, rolling his eyes, shaking his head, and telling me, *You're such a fucking dumbass.*

But the one thing all my gray matter has in common? Every part of me is Into. This. Woman.

I swallow the words stuck in my throat as her body stops moving and she asks, "What did you think?"

What did I think?

I think I'm like every guy in every movie, when the gorgeous friend he's falling for tries on a bunch of outfits and prances around the dressing room and comes out with silly hats and gigantic sunglasses and makes pouty faces, and everybody laughs, and it's all fun and games.

Until that moment at the end, when she emerges wearing a beautiful, stunning, perfect dress and she looks incredible, and says, "What do you think?"

In that moment, his eyes widen and all his wishes flicker across them.

What do I think?

I think this—that it's been a couple days since I met her, but already I'm feeling like the way we talk, the way we connect, the way she is so easy to get along with is making it so much harder for me to stay in Monopoly jail.

Her question echoes in my head while I replay every euphoric moment of that performance. Then in a low, strangled voice, I say, "Nirvana."

She moves to the lip of the stage. "What? I didn't hear you."

As the haze lifts and the buzzing in my body slows, I'm answering so many questions at once.

What do I think of that passionate, ethereal, seductive dance?

How do I feel spending time with this incredible goddess?

What kind of music should they dance to?

"Nirvana," I repeat. "That dance should start with Nirvana."

12

Note to self: should have had the ice cream *after* London danced for me, not before.

Maybe I can find a bucket of ice in this theater.

Or possibly a cold shower. I'll pop in, cool off, and no one will be any the wiser that I'm on fucking fire.

When London hops off the stage, her purse over her shoulder, she grabs my arm, grinning wildly. "Nirvana is brilliant. Is there any chance I can convince you to spend another hour with me and discuss all things grunge rock, you evil genius who's not evil but still a genius?"

Humor. Teasing. Yes, that'll work almost as well as buckets of ice water. "I don't need to be at the radio station for my show till eight, and since it's only four, I could possibly be convinced. But it might require more food at this point," I say, since food will also help distract me from the way she cranked the dial to high on my lust for her.

She lowers her voice to a clandestine whisper.

"Word on the street is *you* can be bribed with a nominal amount of tacos. And I just happen to know a guy."

"A taco dealer? In LA? You've got your ears to the ground," I say, playing along with her.

"Work with me, Teddy."

"I thought that was what we were doing. But you don't have to skimp. A full order works too." We head up the aisle toward the exit.

"Then you shall get a full order," she says, reaching into her purse for her glasses.

"How well can you see without those?" I ask.

She bumps into a chair then laughs. "Just kidding. I can see fine without them, but better with them."

"Good thing you have them, then."

Once outside we grab some carne asada at a truck down the street, and even though it's my second round of tacos today, I do indeed love them that much. We devour our food as we walk and talk, discussing music and dance and friends we depend on.

She tells me about her Woman Power Trio, as she calls them. "Olive bartends in Venice and is obsessed with sexy audiobooks. She's my age but married already. She's bold, brash, and the one person I can call at any hour of the day with a crisis." She stops to take a bite of her taco, and a dab of sauce mars her lip. But before the temptation to wipe it away becomes too strong, she takes care of it for me—with that tongue. That sweet pink tongue.

"Then there's Emery. She's a whip-smart junior TV producer who's been burned by love but keeps on trying. An attitude that has served her well in business too, since she's the fiercest, most determined person I know. She'd give me a kidney, and I'd do the same for her."

"That's pretty much the highest compliment you can give anyone," I say, then I tell her about Sam, and how the guy has come through for me every time I've needed him, even when I didn't know I needed anyone.

Soon, time starts to unwind, the clock ticking closer to evening as we near the market.

Closer to the time when this feels inevitably more like a date. Exactly what it can't be.

I check the time on my phone, wishing the hour wasn't mocking me. But there it is—close to five. A reminder that we're sliding into a dangerous time zone, where night makes it easier to slip up. "I have my radio show tonight. I should go," I say with obvious reluctance.

"Same. But thanks for spending so much time with me," she says as we near a subway entrance. An idea hits me—because why end this yet?—and I gesture to it. "Do you want to Uber together, or take the train?"

Her brown eyes twinkle with mischief, like public transportation is the height of fun. "Confession: I've never taken the train in LA."

My eyes go wide. My jaw drops. "You're a train virgin?"

She gives me a coquettish grin. "I am. Want to deflower me?"

I'm both turned on and amused. I drop an arm around her shoulders. "Has anyone ever told you that you're kind of flirty and goofy at the same time? Also, this is a friendly limb," I say, nodding to the arm I have wrapped around her. "I'm just stating that for the record."

She pats my elbow. "I had an inkling it was an amiable arm. But thanks for the clarification. Also, maybe *you* bring out my flirty side. And my goofy side. I should stop though. Flirting, that is. Should I stop?"

It's a genuine question, but I can hear the underlying plea—*say no.*

"Nah. What's the harm in flirting?"

I know the answer—*plenty*—but ignore it because flirting is too damn fun.

While we wait for the train, we discuss her routine, debating tracks that'll flow from Nirvana to give her routine the poppy, sexy beat she wants. Everything about this day screams *date*, except for the fact that it's not.

"So, about my brother—"

The train screeches into the station, cutting off the rest of her sentence with a deafening squeal.

But those words are enough to underscore the barrier between us. The reason why the train deflowering and the ice cream and the dancing are all we can allow.

Because we can only be . . . budding colleagues?

Ugh. What a fucking annoying word. *Colleagues.*

"Sure. What about him?" The doors slide open, and we grab seats next to each other.

"We're very close, but I haven't told him yet that I'm working with you."

I furrow my brow. Shit. Is this another secret? Secrets are not my jam.

Perhaps sensing my worry, she sets a hand on my arm. And fuck, that feels good, the way her soft palm curls around me. "It's not bad, Teddy. It's that . . ." She dips her head, her hair sliding across her cheek. She swipes it away. "He's kind of protective."

Abort! Abort!

Abandon ship! Activate the escape hatch.

"Not in a bad way," she continues. "Just in an older brother way. Know what I mean?"

That's not reassuring either.

"I have an older sister. And protective isn't how I'd describe Sabrina," I offer with a shrug.

"Hey! I didn't know you had a sister." She lets go of my arm and bounces a little. "I want details."

She legit sounds like my family tree is the most fascinating topic in the universe, and that is endearing as hell. "She lives in Seattle. She's an ER doctor."

"Good for her. That sounds intense."

"That's Sabrina for you. But she's not protective. Mostly, when we were growing up, she liked to tell me I was cute and adorable and so sweet, and could I please sweep the floors, and put away the dishes, and vacuum the carpets?"

"And was she successful at complimenting you into doing her chores?"

"I was hooked and reeled in with hardly a fight. But she learned from the best. To this day, my mom calls and asks me to do basic handiwork around the house— hang a picture on the wall or fix a shelf or whatever—

since my dad's not handy. And she'll say, 'Oh, that was so funny when you did that celebrity impersonation. Can you fix my sink?'"

"It still works?"

"I'm a sucker for flattery," I admit.

"So, basically, telling you that you're a babe will get you to mow my lawn?"

I wiggle my brow. "Yes, London. That's what's required for me to . . . *mow your lawn.*"

Snorting, she covers her mouth with her hand. "That sounds quite dirty."

"So dirty it wouldn't take any compliments. I'd hang out in your lawn all day long for free."

"All night too?" she asks, a naughty glimmer in her eyes.

"Yes. Yes, I would."

She sighs and runs her hand through her hair. "I walked right into that, and now I need to segue back to Archer."

I pull an imaginary hand brake then talk into my hands as though I'm on an amusement park PA system. "And we've now arrived at the end of Innuendo Trail. Please undo your seat belts and make sure you have all your personal belongings. Exit to your left as more flirts make their way onto the car behind you. Your ride is over."

She laughs for several fantastic seconds. "Anyway," she says, tucking a strand of hair behind her ear, "Archer also sees me as the little sister, which of course I am. But he's a look-out-for-her type of guy. And since he's given me this great chance to present a routine for the owners of his club, I want to impress them. To show them I can deliver something amazing and keep Edge on, well, the cutting edge. Plus, I hope this routine will be a stellar addition to my portfolio and attract Andre's attention as well." She looks at me earnestly, as if she's not sure I'll understand. "That's why I wanted to meet with you, make sure this"—she gestures from herself to me—"will work out before I let Archer know about it. He'll be cool, but I wanted to give you the heads-up on the situation. This is a huge opportunity, and I want to do everything right."

All of this is good news for her, for Archer, for the club, and, by extension, me.

But it's also a reminder of the giant roadblock that keeps me sitting here wanting to link our fingers but unable to hold her hand or any other part of her.

"Great. So you'll tell him we're collaborating, and he'll be stoked."

"Definitely. He's pretty busy with meetings, but I'll catch up with him in a day or so."

"Were you guys close growing up?" I might as well quiz her about her relationship with him. It'll keep the issue front and center.

Right where I need it.

"Definitely. He looked out for me, was always weighing in on family talks with Mom and Dad. He took it quite seriously. Like what school I should go to, what sports I should play, what classes I should take. And so on."

"Did you like that?"

"It was eye-roll-inducing as a tween, but looking

back, I love that he always had my best interests at heart. That he wanted to be involved. My parents are like that too. They even had matching jackets from my cheerleading and dance team days and used to wear them to my competitions. Now they break them out whenever I come over. They're still together after thirty-five years."

"Goals. That's awesome. And they live here?"

"They do. I'm having dinner with them tomorrow night."

That makes me ridiculously happy. Sure, Tracy was close to her dad, but they both always bad-mouthed her mom. That should have been a big red flag. Nice to see London likes and respects both her parents. "Mine live here too. I'm seeing them next week."

"Birds of a feather," she says in a soft voice that hints she likes that we've got the same plumage.

Soon, we reach our stop, and as we exit the station, I raise my face to the fading sun. Here we are at the end of another . . . almost date.

Saying goodbye to the woman I like a whole hell of a lot.

Fate, you can fuck off.

I walk her home, and when we reach her house, Mr. Darcy is outside cavorting with two guys I recognize as her friends from the club, the ones who look like they could be on the cover of any celebrity magazine in the world.

"Do you live with Tom Ellis and John David Washington?"

London laughs. "I know, right? Everyone in LA is

ridiculously beautiful. Tom Ellis is Eli, and John David Washington is Nate."

The A-list look-alikes are watering the lawn. Only in LA.

As London's shoes slap the sidewalk, the butterscotch-colored Chihuahua mix loses his mind with glee, darting over to her at the speed of sound.

"My little love," she says, scooping him up and peppering him with kisses as he wags his tail like it's a propeller.

She clutches the dog in her arms as she gestures to her friends. "Guys, this is Teddy. Teddy, this is Nate and Eli."

Nate arches a teasing brow and meets London's gaze. "Ah, the guy you had dinner with last night, who kisses like a rock star?"

Beet. Red.

Wait—that's inaccurate. She turns every shade of red in the color wheel, and I want to thump my chest.

London narrows her eyes. "You're evil, and we're not friends anymore."

Eli laughs and drapes an arm around his partner. "Nate, love, did you forget? She also called him the total hottie with the sexy voice and yummy eyes and lips that she couldn't get enough of."

Eli flashes a devilish grin at London. Yup, Eli is pure Tom Ellis at his Lucifer best, and he sounds like Ellis too, with a proper British accent and all.

Nate elbows him. "Look at you, showing off with your perfect memory of how London described the man."

London points at them each in turn. "You're both officially out of my will."

The guys laugh, then Eli says to me, "Nice to meet you, Teddy."

We exchange hellos, and London offers to drive me home. "Plus, I need to escape from these two before they serve up more of my secrets," she says.

"Or before *you* do," Eli adds, as London grabs her keys from her pocket. Her car is parked on the street, so she opens the back door, tucks Mr. Darcy into a dog car seat, then buckles him in.

Yeah, that's not totally fucking adorable.

I get into the passenger seat, and she drives me to my place, pulling into the lot of my condo.

"Thanks again," I say, unbuckling my seat belt.

"You're most welcome," she says, unclipping the dog. "He doesn't like to stay in the back seat unless I'm driving."

"And he should have everything he wants."

"You get me. Thank you," she says, as the dog folds himself into a dog ball on her lap, looking like a contented prince.

Well, he *is* in her lap.

"Also, can we rewind to that moment on your front lawn?" I ask, a smirk tugging at my lips.

"I don't know. Can we?" she tosses back.

"So I kiss like a rock star?"

She rolls her eyes. "Well, yeah. You were there last night. Don't you think you kiss like a rock star?"

I laugh. "I'm more interested in what *you* think of my

kissing. And I'm so not thinking about kissing you again," I lie.

What I'm really not thinking about is about work.

Or her brother.

Or the tangled webs we weave.

I'm not even thinking too much about the fact that I need to jet in twenty minutes to get to the radio station in time.

Because when the woman you're into tells her buds she can't get enough of you, everything else falls by the wayside.

The second she removes her glasses, the moment shifts. I take her face in my hands and give in again.

As the sun dips toward the ocean, I forget about all the roadblocks, because I'm the guy she told her friends about. I like being that guy right now.

Because that guy has his hands on London.

I bring her closer, clasp harder, and slide my tongue across her lips. Her soft, lush, fantastic-tasting lips.

Especially when they part for me, when she lets out a needy murmur and draws me closer, even with her dog in her lap.

Following her cues, I deepen the kiss—with lips, with hands, with contact, moving closer in the cramped space of the car.

I slide a hand through her hair as the moment amps up, and we kiss harder, hungrier.

It's next-level kissing—teeth nipping at lips, tongues exploring, bodies inching toward more delicious, devouring territory.

Her hands travel to my stomach, sliding under my shirt and up my abs to my pecs.

She stops there, curling them over my chest, but I don't want to stop. I want to bring her inside my home, undress her, and explore her.

Except those lines are so much riskier than *this* one.

This one in the car in a parking lot.

This one that can only go so far.

Because I can't go too far.

Or I'll do something *stupider*.

For now, stupid is enough. Stupid like pretending this fantastic, mind-numbing kiss doesn't break the rules we set last night.

I stay here, my hands roping through her hair, my tongue tangoing with hers, her scent going to my head.

I don't want to end the kiss, and I don't think she does either.

But a small, soft tongue licks my face.

And it's not hers.

I laugh, and we break apart—panting, turned on, and totally cracking up about the dog getting in on the action.

"So we're just going to pretend that was, like, an extension kiss," I offer after we catch our breath.

"Of yesterday's?"

"Exactly," I say.

"And it won't happen again," she says, intensely serious.

"It absolutely won't. And I won't be thinking of undoing this shirt," I say, unclicking her seat belt then tugging lightly at the soft cotton, sliding my hand under it, letting my fingers trace her skin.

She gasps as I journey across her soft stomach, savoring the feel of her flesh for the first time.

My fingers are on a mission—slide higher, travel farther, discover the lush lands of London.

Ah, hell. What's one more kiss?

With my hand firmly on the pert mound of her breast, I return to her lips and kiss her harder, my head a hazy, static blur of lust and desire. My body hums with the need to crank the seat back, pull her on top of me, and say *fuck everything* so I can fuck her.

I tug at her waist, gripping her hip, yanking her close.

London slides on top of me, straddling me, and I run my hands up her back, hauling her in for a hot full-body kiss. I want to spend the rest of the night with her like this, on top of me, here in her car, our bodies grinding.

My hands travel down to her ass, gripping those tight, firm cheeks and dragging her closer. She rocks against the ridge of my erection, and my bones vibrate with lust, my brain going hazy with desire. She breathes out hard then kisses harder, pressing and pushing.

London is hungry and confident, and it's so damn sexy.

I rub against her as her breathing grows more erratic, like maybe, just maybe, she could come like this.

As soon as that tantalizing thought flicks through my head, I imagine London's noises, her expressions, the telltale signs that she's close.

Will I be lucky enough to discover those signs?

Will they become part of my London lexicon?

I'd like to know them all.

Especially since this kiss in the front seat of her car has gone from zero to sixty in seconds, and I want to see how much further it can go.

I run a hand along her arm, and she feels like . . . *fur*.

What the hell?

I yank apart from London to find Mr. Darcy pumping her arm.

I groan. "Umm."

"Mr. Darcy! You naughty boy."

She grabs him, but he's still humping air as she returns to the driver's seat.

I have no choice but to laugh. I'm pretty sure I'm going to die of busting a gut, and London might too, because she is slumped against the steering wheel, gasping for air, when the dog finally stops moving his doggie hips.

"I forgot to tell you. My dog's breed is actually *horn*," she says.

"London, all dogs are horns, but yours seems to be the rare subbreed: cockblocker. Though maybe we needed his *kissus interruptus*."

She brings her hand to her face. "I know we're not supposed to be doing that. But you're irresistible." She juts out her chin, owning it, then strokes the horn dog. "Thank you, Mr. Darcy, for being a cockblocker." She drops a kiss onto his soft head, and he lets his tongue loll out.

"Yeah, thanks, I think," I say with a laugh, then I turn serious. "But really, I should behave."

"I should too. No matter how irresistible you are. This is a big chance for me in my career, and I've worked hard, so I will not be distracted by your lips."

"I'll try not to let them get in the way of yours again."

"Thanks. I'd appreciate that," she says with a smile.

"Let's make a pact. No more rogue kissing." I offer her a hand.

She takes it and shakes. "We will have each other's backs. Focus on work and on taking Edge to the next level. For both of our careers. All rogue kissing must end."

I go inside, feed my dog, and take him for a walk before I head to the station, weirdly grateful that her dog saved my ass.

But kind of ungrateful too.

Because holy fuck.

That kiss. Those hands. *That woman.*

13

An hour later

From the Woman Power Trio, aka the text messages of London and her two besties, Olive and Emery

Emery: Where's my full report?

Olive: Because we're betting you caved. Drinks are on me if I'm wrong.

London: And if you're right?

Olive: Drinks are on you, obvs.

London: I'm not paying for drinks at your bar, Liv.

Olive: You don't have to, Dancing Queen. We're at Speakeasy. It's maybe a mile from your house. Get your cute butt over here and tell us everything about your elbow-licking *work, work, work* non-date.

London: If you insist. I just finished walking my main man, so I'll see you in thirty.

Emery: Give us a hint though. Did you cave again?

London: Does kissing count as caving?

Olive: On every planet, woman. On literally every planet.

London: Then drinks are on me. And I'm hoping the willpower will be on the two of you, because I need it, friends. Desperately. Gimme some of yours?

Emery: *activates pep talk gene* *prepares to impart epic advice and willpower*

Olive: We will not let you fail. Your career goals are too important to be distracted by hot lips. Think of us as your life coaches. Prepare for all sorts of wisdom and wine.

* * *

Three hours later

London: That was mostly wine. Not wisdom. You spent the whole time asking what I liked about him and encouraging me to see him when I'm done with this work project. You suck.

Olive: We love you too.

Emery: We can't help it if we're problem solvers.

London: Making plans for when we aren't working together won't solve a thing. He's so not available for so many reasons. Make me stop thinking about him.

Olive: I've got this! Have I told you about this new audiobook I picked up where the heroine is into threesomes?

London: How exactly will threesomes help my cause? My dog already tried to have a threesome with Teddy and me.

Olive: Threesomes won't help. But books will. Just listen to this hot tamale, and it'll take your mind off the guy you can't have and won't see again because you're going to be such a good girl. Here's a snippet from Dax Long, my fave narrator.

"You can take it, kitten. You can handle both of us at the same time. That's right. Just relax. You feel us now?"

London: Ugh, he sounds like Teddy. Not helping!

Olive: Teddy sounds like my favorite audiobook narrator? I'm so jelly now.

London: Good night, crazy girl.

Olive: Good night, Dancing Queen.

14

It's Thursday night. We have three hen parties in the building, and Archer is like a general giving his troops our final marching orders.

"All right, gentlemen. The Rothman party is already seated," he says as he paces the dressing room backstage. "That bride-to-be is an entertainment executive named Bloom, and she's wearing a sash that says 'My friends made me wear this.' She's a good friend of one of my sister's roomies."

I almost ask, *Nate or Eli?* But I catch myself and zip my lips because I shouldn't know her roomies.

I keep my insider knowledge of London's life locked up airtight as Archer continues, "The maid of honor tells me Bloom has a thing for Aussie men. Sam, you know what to do. Play it up."

"No worries, mate," Sam says, doing his best down under accent. "Even though I won't be the one up there doing my best Hugh Jackman impression. Teddy will."

"Someone has to do the talking," I say.

"And someone has to have the *moves*," Sam says.

"And we all have a division of labor to keep the show moving," says Archer. "Then, we have Mallory and her guests at the bar. And she happens to love firemen."

"I've got a hose right here for her," Carlos offers with a pump of his built-like-a-Marine hips. He has close-cropped brown hair to match, and the look works for the job.

Archer rolls his eyes, and holy hell—they're the same fucking color as London's. I'm not okay with that.

"Keep it classy," he says. "This is a revue, not a strip club."

"I tell my boyfriend the same thing whenever he gets jelly about me baring it all," Carlos says.

"You don't bare it all," Archer says.

"I know, but I like to keep him on his toes."

And I'm not thinking about London's eyes anymore.

"Then we have the Flashmans. They'll be arriving in around thirty minutes. Bride's name is Victoria, and Miss Victoria loves a man in uniform."

Carlos licks his lips. "Me too."

"Again, Carlos," Archer says.

"What? It's true. I mean, have you seen those hot cop videos?"

"No, I have not," Archer says.

"Well, try them sometime."

That earns him another eye roll.

Another *well-deserved* eye roll.

"Wait," Stanley cuts in, raising his hand like he's in class. "Are we doing the handcuffs number or the soldier number? Which men in uniform are we talking about? Because there are a lot of uniforms out there in the world. Postal workers have uniforms too."

"Yes, Stanley. We know your day job is delivering mail," Sam says.

"And his night job is delivering . . . *male*," Carlos says with a salacious wink.

Archer slow claps. "Yes, puns are always entertaining. But back to business." He turns to me. "You got everything, Teddy?"

"Hot accents, hot hoses, Carlos likes cops and playing jealousy games. Stanley delivers all the packages. You enjoy homophones. It's all in my notes." I rattle it off at a steady clip without missing a beat. "Also, yes, I have music for that."

"Sam, Stanley, Carlos—I need a ton of energy out of you three tonight. Keep it classy, but a little dirty, like a proper martini should be," Archer says.

The four of us laugh, but the chuckles do nothing to take the edge off the tension in every cell in my body. It's been three days since I last saw London, and I'm not sure if Archer knows we've hung out. Has she told him yet that we're working together? Does he know we had ice cream?

"You've got this, guys," Archer says, giving us his *go, team, go* grin, which twists my stomach. Why the hell can't he be an asshole? That would make my life so much easier.

Though not really.

Who wants to work for a dick?

Which means . . . rock, meet hard place. I am in you.

Ten minutes later, the lights dim, and I lure the

crowd in with a fucking awesome Australian accent as Men at Work's "Down Under" begins to play. "G'day, ladies, and welcome to Edge. We found our first act of the evening out back. Please give it up for Crocodile Hump Me."

Sam struts onstage in skintight dungarees and a wide-brimmed hat, which he tosses to our first bride of the night, Bloom. And like that, we find our rhythm as the rest of the guys join him onstage for the dance number. My nerves disappear as I let all thoughts of London and Archer fade away. I focus on the show and giving the crowd what they want, and the next few hours fly by.

* * *

When the guys finish their *Top Gun*–themed grand finale, complete with aviators, bomber jackets, and little else, I throw on the post-show playlist and head backstage to check in.

With a look of terror in his eyes, Sam beckons me over. "Dude. Boss wants to see you."

The floor falls out from under me.

Oh, shit.

He found out about London.

She told him we kissed more than once. Once can be forgiven. Once is an error. But twice is on purpose. He's protective. He's going to fire me.

Because rogue kissing is not acceptable.

I shouldn't have crossed the line.

With nerves frayed to the edge, I begin the death march to his office.

"Do you think he knows?" Sam whispers, his voice thin with worry.

"He probably has a camera in London's car. Brothers do that, right? Maybe he saw me kissing her in her car the other day."

"That's normal. I bet that sounds exactly like what he'd do." He smacks my arm. "Seriously, do you think she told him you're banging her?"

I snap my gaze to him. "I'm not banging her."

"But you want to."

"But I didn't."

"There's a thin line between kissing and banging."

I stare at him like he's grown antlers. "It's not a thin line. It's a thick one. A huge one. A highway-median-sized one. There are a ton of lines between kissing and banging."

"All amazing lines," Sam says, suddenly on my side again.

"None of which I've crossed," I hiss as I turn the corner, the sound of Archer's laughter drifting into the hall and gutting me.

"Good luck. I'll say I knew you when," Sam says, cringing. "I can't watch horror movies, so I've got to jet."

I've never been a fan of scary films either, but seems I bought this ticket, and now I'll have to face what's on the big screen.

15

I walk the plank into Archer's office and then stop, my eyes all but springing out of my head like a cartoon character's.

London is here.

She's standing next to Archer, checking out a picture on his phone. She jerks her gaze over to meet mine and tries to say something with her eyes.

Like maybe she's pointing to my pocket. My phone?

Did she send me a message?

I didn't check my phone.

I'll have to improvise.

"Teddy, I have a bone to pick with you," Archer says, a serious glint in his eyes.

And that's the end of my job.

The end of paying my bills.

The end of my condo.

I'll be out on the street with Bowie tomorrow.

I gulp but say nothing.

"Isn't it time for *you* to fess up?" he asks, still staunchly serious.

London rolls her eyes. "Archer, dramatic much?"

He gives her a look. "I could say the same to you, missy."

"Oh my God, you're not Dad. Don't call me missy."

I can't tell if she's laughing at him, me, or whatever was on his phone. God, I hope it was a cat GIF. *May she please have been laughing at a cat GIF.*

I don't move. I stand there, waiting for the guillotine. It's coming.

Three, two, one.

Archer gestures to the gorgeous woman I've already kissed. More than once. "This is my sister, London."

"Yes, we've met," I blurt out.

Why did I just serve that up?

Because that's what almost dead men do.

"Don't you have something to tell me?" Archer asks pointedly.

I kissed your sister, and it was fucking awesome. Then I kissed her again, and it was more awesome.

Instead, I shrug. It's all I got.

London points at Archer. "You need to stop." She looks at me. "He's being an *annoying big brother*."

Archer laughs, drapes an arm around London, then jams his knuckles into her hair, rubbing affectionately hard.

And yeah.

I can't kiss her again.

Ever.

Because he's such a big brother.

And she's such a little sister.

And this is such a big mess.

"She told me she enlisted you to help her develop the routine to show the partners. That's an awesome idea." Archer grins, looking from her to me. "Such a great idea, I wish I'd thought of it myself."

What?

He's not canning me for kissing his sister?

He's not raking me over the coals for grazing his sister's rack?

I can breathe again.

"She's brilliant. I'm telling you, she is brilliant," Archer says with obvious pride.

"She is. She's completely brilliant," I say, grateful to be able to tell the truth.

This is why I hate mixing business with pleasure. I don't want to lie. Juggling multiple stories is not my jam. I don't even like jam. I'm more of a peanut butter guy.

And I don't want to risk my job.

I keep talking so I don't do other things with my mouth, like seal it to hers. "The whole idea is brilliant. What you have planned for the club. Adding more dancing. Some new numbers. I bet it'll draw even more crowds," I say, leaning into the vision. "It's important to broaden our reach and explore new markets. Great time to be expanding too."

"Exactly. It's like you can read my mind," Archer says.

I only hope he can't read *my* mind, because if he could, it would look like a spilled bag of Scrabble tiles that spell *I really like your sister and I need to get the fuck out of here.*

Because my brain is at war with my body, twin desires tugging me in opposite directions.

I want to tell Archer I have feelings for his sister and get everything out in the open. I want to run away and pretend this meeting never happened.

But before I can do any of those things, Archer chimes in again. "Have you two ironed out a set list for her new material? You should get together ASAP to discuss what might work best. If this goes well, the owners will want to get this up and running stat."

Yes.

This is brilliant.

At least he knows I'm hanging out with her.

Oh, wait. Hanging out with her is what tempts me TO TOUCH HER ALL THE FUCK OVER.

What the hell have I gotten myself into?

Except Archer got me into it. So now I need to get myself through this.

I need to meet her someplace safe.

Someplace that won't tempt me.

And I know exactly where that is.

"What if we meet *here* during the day?" I suggest. There is zero that is tempting about this joint.

"Or you could meet at the radio station. Weren't you telling me that it has a great digital collection and speaker setup?"

Yeah, and it has a fucking couch too. Thanks a lot, Archer.

I gulp and then fasten on a smile. "Yes. Perfect."

"Excellent. Now I need to chat with Carlos and Stanley about a booking for tomorrow night," Archer says. Sure enough, those guys are just outside and head into his office as I leave.

On my way down the hall, I check my phone to find a text from London sent an hour ago.

London: Heads-up! I'm at the club. Archer loves the idea of us collaborating! Yay!

Yay.

So much not yay.

I have to ignore this powder keg of feelings I have for London.

Because this is about work. This can only be about work.

* * *

I open the door to my car, when the unmistakable sound splits my eardrums.

Shrieking.

Squealing.

Then a woman's voice. "Oh my God! You are *just* the guy I wanted to see!"

That doesn't sound like the opening line of an ax murderer who's about to hack you to pieces in a parking lot.

At least, I hope not.

And the woman click-clacking across the parking lot in a black dress and white sash isn't wielding an ax. Just a tiara. So, odds are good I'll end the night with my limbs still attached.

Bloom, the entertainment exec bachelorette, charges at me in a feat worthy of a new Olympic sport—rushing across concrete in high heels while smashed. Come to think of it, running anywhere in high heels should be an Olympic sport because that's world-class athletic prowess, wasted or not.

Five seconds of ear-piercing shrieks later, she slams her hands down on my shoulders. "DJ Insomnia! I was hoping to catch you."

I have no idea what she's talking about, but I go with it. "Cool. That's me. DJ Insomnia, your first choice to make a party last. What can I do ya for?"

She flicks a strand of dark hair off her cheek, her lip gloss smeared, the scent of margaritas swirling around her like it's her new perfume. "You're never going to believe this. I have the worst news ever. The worst of all the worst news that was ever delivered anywhere."

"That doesn't sound very good," I say dryly, waiting to see where this conversation is going. My guess is Wedding Town, because the rest of the bridal party marches across the parking lot to flank their bridal leader in what feels like a *Reservoir Dogs* meets *Bridesmaids* moment.

"But see, it's not the worst news. Because my gals and I—we were discussing it. And we texted Nate. And we had the best idea. All of us. It's the best idea ever." She takes a tequila-scented pause. "Be my Obi-Wan."

I arch an inquiring brow. "Is this a you're-my-only-hope request?"

Synchronized shrieking commences.

"OMG, he knows what I mean."

The maid of honor jumps up and down. A bridesmaid claps.

"If you could be my Obi-Wan, I would just kiss you. I mean, I won't kiss you, because I totally love my husband. Well, he's not my husband yet. He's going to be my husband in three days, and I'm not going to kiss anybody else, but if I did, it would be you as long as you tell me that you can do one thing for me."

"What would that thing be?"

"My DJ backed out of my wedding. He booked a shampoo commercial, and it shoots this weekend. It's a national, so obvs, he can't miss it," she says.

I feel my luck changing on a dime. I can guess what's coming next from Bloom, and in three, two, one, it arrives. "And Nate said London told him you also do weddings. So, would you please DJ at my wedding this Sunday?"

There is only one answer. "Yes."

16

I meet with Bloom Friday morning at Doctor Insomnia's Tea and Coffee Emporium, not only because I like the name, but because it's in Silverlake, between both of us. Over a vanilla latte for her and a black coffee for me, we review her picks for the first dance, the dance with her father, and the groom's dance with his mom.

She also rattles off all her favorite numbers and her never-ever-play-at-my-wedding list.

"No 'Macarena,' no 'Every Breath You Take,' and no 'My Heart Will Go On,'" she says, counting off on her fingers.

"Because it's cheesy, because it's a stalker song, and because no one wants to think of Leonardo DiCaprio dying."

The bride-to-be's grin is massive. "It's like it was meant to be, you deejaying my wedding."

"Kismet," I say, feeling great about this opportunity. "Glad I could help out."

She gives me the rest of the venue and timeline details, and I tell her I'll see her on Sunday.

When I hop into my car, my phone buzzes with a text. Apparently, I'm Pavlov's dog, because the possibility that it might be from London has me swiping the screen faster than usual.

But I've got too much riding on my career to get sidetracked now, especially with new opportunities like Bloom's wedding in my future.

I'll be friendly and businesslike if it's London. But my mom's name pops up on the screen.

Mom: Ready when you are.

Since I haven't heard from her in a few days, this text must be for someone else, so I use this as an excuse to call.

"Hi, Teddy. Good to hear from you."

"Question, Mom. Ready for what? Chess? Mahjongg? Key party?"

"Oops, did I send that to you? I meant to text your father. We're brunching. Day date."

"You text him even though you live in the same house?"

"We're a modern couple. Don't be so surprised we know how to text."

I shake my head. "That wasn't the surprise. It was that you didn't just yell up the stairs."

"We like to text." Do I hear a hint of coyness in her voice?

"Okay, then. Carry on."

"We will. We like to text about a lot of things."

I cringe, even though my parents have always been a touchy-feely couple. Which I truly don't mind. I just don't require *details*. "Mom, I don't need to know that."

"Hush. You weren't made in a test tube."

"Still don't need to know that you and Dad *like to text*."

"I didn't say what we texted about," she says, all faux demure.

"Yes, but I got the picture."

She scoffs. "We don't send pics. That's too risqué. Please tell me you don't send dirty pics to women."

"Mom!"

"You're still my son, and I'll still look out for you."

"I don't send dirty pics. I'm not even seeing anyone."

"That's a shame. We can try to find a nice girl to bring to the cages on Monday for batting practice."

I groan. The last thing I want is a blind double date with my parents. Sure, I love them, and I get a kick out of going to Dad's softball games, where Mom brings him orange slices like she did for me when I was a kid.

But a blind date?

No, thanks.

"Call me crazy, but seeing the two of you is enough for me. And do me a favor, Mom?"

"Sure."

"Double-check before you send me a text meant for Dad."

She takes a beat, then says, "Think before texting. Those are some words to live by."

Words to live by indeed.

And I do just that all day as I resist the urge to text London. I also keep my eye on the prize while working at Edge that night.

Bills fly across the stage. Women cheer. The music pounds.

And the tips are the best they've ever been.

It's a great Friday night.

As I make my way out of the club, Archer's behind the bar, working on his laptop, probably tallying up receipts.

He tips his chin in my direction. "I heard the news."

I flinch, my skin prickling with nerves. Is he toying with me like he did with London? I toss out a curveball. "That the Dodgers are leading the division with one month to go?"

Please tell me he's talking about baseball.

"That is indeed excellent news. But I meant about Bloom."

Is he pissed I'm doing business with a customer? That's not against the rules though. Plus, Archer knows about my side-hustle plans. He's never had an issue with it before.

"You heard about her wedding?" I ask carefully, since I'm not sure what's coming next.

"One of her friends forgot her phone, so they came back in last night, and Bloom was talking about having nabbed you last minute for her wedding. That's great. Good to see you growing your business."

I breathe a sigh of relief. "I'm stoked. I met with her earlier today about the music she likes. Should be a good event."

"Definitely. London says Bloom knows how to throw a party."

My head spins in a complete 360. "London said that?" I croak. Why would London say that?

"She was telling me the other night that she's going to the wedding. With Nate, since Eli has to go out of town for work."

Right. Bloom was here at Edge in the first place because of Nate.

And now London is going to be at the wedding.

But there will be no rogue kissing.

Hell, how could there be? I'll be at the DJ booth, and she'll be with Nate.

So, I'll behave. It'll be easy.

So. Damn. Easy.

"Then I'm looking forward to the wedding even more." I hastily add, "Since London said it'll be a good gig. That's why I'm looking forward to it."

No other reason, of course.

Archer tilts his head, his expression serious. "But should I be looking for a new deejay?"

"What?" I jerk my head back. "No. Why?"

He drags his palm across his forehead in exaggerated relief. "Whew. Good. Because I don't want to lose you when you become the city's most sought-after wedding deejay. Finding a good deejay is harder than finding good dancers. A six-pack, some stage presence, and a few solid moves aren't hard to come by in this town.

But someone with encyclopedic knowledge of tunes, who's quick on his feet with a quip and a comment? That's hard to replace."

A smile breaks out. "I'll be sticking around for a while." Especially since I want that raise. Because . . . *bills*. "Maybe not forever, but for now. No worries there. Just trying to grow my side business at the same time."

"Makes sense. You want options for the long-term. Just do me a favor?"

"Sure," I say, hoping it's something I can deliver.

"Give me a heads-up if anything changes, okay? So I can look for a replacement?"

That feels like the least I can do. "Of course," I say, my shoulders relaxing.

He gestures to his laptop. "I've got a ton of work to finish before I go on this corporate camping retreat."

I tilt my head. "Corporate and camping? That sounds like an oxymoron."

"You're telling me. I've got to work even later to go on an unplugged retreat . . . about work. Maybe we'll eat nothing but jumbo shrimp."

"That's seriously . . . funny."

"I see what you did there. Not bad, Teddy. But I'm sure I'll learn tons, so there's that."

"Let's at least hope the s'mores are good."

"There's always the s'mores." He nods toward the door. "See you tomorrow."

I take off, grateful to be needed. Glad everything is all good.

At home, I take Bowie for a long walk, checking out the science podcast London recommended.

I learn about toasters and decide filaments are cool. When I go to bed, I chalk up a win—I've navigated another day without lusting over London. And as if to prove myself to the universe, I text her, suggesting she meet me after my show at the station on Monday night so we can continue our strictly professional arrangement.

Yep, I'm rocking this resistance. Rocking it like Springsteen rocks, well, everything.

I go full Boss the next day too, working out with Sam, catching up on the news, chatting with Sherri *en español*, then listening to another episode of the science podcast. Before I head to the club, a fantastic email lands on my phone. One of the community groups I emailed needs a DJ for an awards ceremony, so I say yes and add that to my calendar for early next month.

Finally, I head to the club for a raucous Saturday night.

By the time midnight rolls around, I've conducted a London detox.

Pretty damn impressive.

But when she texts me, my resistance gets up, walks out the door, and deserts me entirely.

All that's left is my desire to get to know the most fascinating woman I've ever met.

And to know her in every damn way.

17

A few minutes earlier

From the Woman Power Trio, aka the text messages of London and her two besties, Olive and Emery

Emery: Just text him.

Olive: You know you want to.

London: You're such enablers.

Emery: You say that like it's a bad thing.

London: It *is* a bad thing. For many reasons. I told you the reasons.

Olive: Reasons, schmeasons. Besides, you have research to do.

Emery: And we do want to know if our theory holds up.

London: So I'm your lab rat?

Olive: You're too cute to be a lab rat. Also, I'm against animal testing.

London: Yes, me too.

Emery: Same, obvs. But we don't want you to be a lab rat. We want you to be a lab woman who goes out and gets it, girl.

Olive: I mean, in your libido's defense, it's been a while.

London: So you're looking out for my sex life, or lack thereof?

Emery: I think that's quite a noble calling.

Olive: I concur. Now, go forth and text. In the name of research.

London: I'll just text to say hi. That's all. I'm *not* texting for other reasons.

Emery: Whatever you need to tell yourself to sleep at night.

London: ENABLER!

Olive: AND YOU LOVE IT!

18

After work, I melt into the couch with a bowl of dandan noodles, Bowie cuddled next to me. Just as I'm about to dive into this peanuty goodness, my phone vibrates in my pocket.

It's a text. From London. After midnight.

Okay, Teddy, relax. Put the chopsticks down and read the message.

London: Hey, you!

Maybe it's the *hey, you* that does it—the easy conversational vibe, but also the intimacy of it. Or maybe I'm reading too much into it.

Or maybe I just like the woman too much for my own good.

Teddy: Hey to you too.

London: I hope it's not too late to text.

Teddy: I'm a night owl.

London: Whew. Good. Did you just get off?

My fingers move faster than my brain, and the text is on its way before I have a chance to second-guess myself.

Teddy: Yes, but I was thinking of you the whole time.

But before I can castigate myself any further, a reply pops up on the screen.

London: I was asking about WORK, but it's nice to hear you're thinking of me . . .

I kind of can't *stop* thinking of her. Even when I was trying to, she was there in the back of my brain.

London: Just checking in about Monday. Are we all set to meet at the station after your show?

Teddy: Sam is lined up to walk the dogs, so I'm good for the night. No need to rush.

London: Dogs? I thought you just had Bowie.

Teddy: I do, but I walk my neighbor's dog when I can. Sherri is older and not as mobile as she used to be, so I try to give her pooch some outdoor time.

London: Aww . . . that's sweet of you.

Teddy: Sherri is awesome, and Bowie loves her beagle rescue Vin Scully, so it all works out.

London: I'm guessing you're being modest here. You sound like you might be a—gasp—good guy.

Teddy: And what leads you to that conclusion?

London: Rescue pittie? Check. Helping little old lady neighbors? Check. Likes his parents? Check. Adds up to a good guy.

I repeat the text out loud, then look at David Bowie. "Does she think being a good guy is bad, buddy? Did I miss a memo?"

Bowie offers his belly but no advice. Typical. I give him a scratch, since he asked nicely—like a good guy.

I take a bite of the noodles, hoping she's not one of

those women who likes jerks. But that doesn't track with her. Time to throw down the simple truth.

Teddy: Sure. I'll own it. Good guy and proud of it.

London: I thought you might be. We were having a debate about good guys versus bad boys at our board game night.

Teddy: I'll bite. What was the debate? Also, who's we?

London: Emery, Olive, Eli, Nate, and myself. You met the guys already. And I told you about my gals. Olive's the married one who loves audiobooks. I'm pretty sure she uses them as foreplay for the sex she and her motor-cycle-riding tattoo artist of a hubby have every night. His name's Hawke, so he couldn't be anything but a bad boy. Emery has a penchant for smooth-talking suits who turn out to be secretly married. I'm trying to cure her of that. And so are Nate and Eli. They're all for good guys. Because, they—wait for it—are good guys. Also, I'm pretty sure they have sex twice a day.

I show the text to Bowie. "We're talking sex now. That's promising, right?"

He thumps his tail.

Wait. Shit. No. I shouldn't talk sex with a woman I want to have sex with but *can't* have sex with.

But that's like taunting a dog with a tennis ball and not throwing it for him.

Like a dog, I chase it.

Teddy: Good for them. Seems like the key to happiness.

London: Yes. Seems to be. You met them. They're the happiest people I know.

Teddy: Scientific studies have shown happiness is a by-product of sex on the reg. Twice daily, in fact.

London: I do believe I've seen those studies too. 😊 But here's the thing . . .

Uh-oh. Like its cousin *but*, nothing good ever comes after *here's the thing.* I jump on the grenade.

Teddy: Here's the thing, what? Good sex is better than ice cream?

London: That depends on the ice cream.

Teddy: Depends on the sex.

London: That may be true. But what I was saying is this: Emery and Olive—already world-wise before they even hit thirty—claimed that only bad boys are good in bed.

Teddy: And good guys are . . . what? Awesome? Incredible? Fucking amazing? Way better than bad boys? I hope you defended the honor of good guys in bed!

She's silent. Well, text silent. But the dots are moving. Then they stop. C'mon, London.

I look at Bowie. "What do you think, buddy? On the one paw, she mentioned sex. On the other paw, she thinks I might be bad at it." He says nothing, but I know what he's thinking. *We can't let this happen.* Fuck it. I can't wait for her response. I keep going.

Teddy: I can't believe you'd allow your friends to talk trash about good guys!

London: I didn't say I agreed with them! I don't *want* to agree with them. But I have no empirical data, Teddy.

Teddy: You've never been with a good guy? Please don't tell me you like jerks or assholes.

London: My last boyfriend was sort of . . . *nice enough.* And honestly, before that, I mostly dated . . . well . . . *not nice guys.* Let's leave it at that.

Teddy: So you don't actually have any data to draw from?

London: I don't! Isn't that terrible?

Teddy: Awful. I bet you wanted to contribute your insight to the debate.

London: I so did. Especially because Olive said it's a scientific fact that nice guys are bad in bed.

Teddy: Olive is wrong.

London: She said it's Newton's fourth law of thermo-dude-namics. A man can be two of these, but never all three: hot, nice, good in bed. And you're obviously hot, and now I'm finding out you're nice, so . . .

Damn, it feels good to hear her call me hot. But she's leaving those ellipses dangling on the end of that text like a gauntlet thrown at my feet. I'm so caught up in this moment, so caught up in her, that I pick that glove right up.

Teddy: Sounds a bit more like a hypothesis than a law to me.

London: Hmm. Good point. And hypotheses do need to be tested. Did you have an experiment in mind?

Teddy: The kind where we'd need to run multiple tests to ensure the accuracy of our results.

London: I do like the sound of multiples.

Teddy: Me too.

I'm burning up everywhere. I head to the refrigerator to grab a seltzer because this interaction with London requires a cooldown.

I return to the couch, staring at the screen. The ball is in my court.

This feels like a challenge. The good-guy challenge. And I'm not sure I can refuse it.

But am I ready to throw my personal rules and guidelines out the window?

I flash back to Archer and our conversation last night.

I flash forward to tomorrow and the wedding.

The wedding London's attending too.

I groan, wanting her, and wanting to resist her.

Which side will win?

I don't have a clue.

All I know is I can't wait to see her again.

Teddy: See you tomorrow at the wedding. I'll be the guy with the headphones on, resisting rogue-kissing the prettiest woman there.

London: I'll be the girl resisting rogue-kissing the DJ. After all, we made a pact.

And I'm going to do my damnedest to honor it.

19

The first thing I do when I'm out of bed the next morning is check my texts, feeling a little like Bowie nudging his nose in the dog food bowl in the early a.m., hoping kibble will magically appear.

But there aren't any new texts from the city's sexiest woman, so my guy and I hit the trails for a morning hike.

An hour, several checks of my phone, and some hard-earned sweat later, I understand my dog a whole lot more.

Staring at the dog food bowl *can* reap rewards.

Because check this out.

I'm the lucky recipient not only of a text from London, but a video file.

Lifting my face to the sky, I offer a silent prayer to all the dirty gods and goddesses. *Let this be a video of her stripping down to nothing . . .*

Wait. Nope. That's so uncouth of me. Truth is, I'd be happy to watch a video of London brushing her teeth.

As soon as that thought hits my brain, another one slams into it like one car rear-ending another.

You've got it bad for this woman if you want to see her brushing her teeth.

Shaking my head at my runaway thoughts, I mutter, "No shit, self. Also, fuck off—fresh breath is cool. Right, Bowie?"

My furry friend tilts his head, his tongue lolling out.

"Good," I say as I make my way down the final bend in the trail, clicking open the video clip.

And happy Sunday morning to me.

This is way better than good dental hygiene.

London: I'm in the studio this morning. Feeling all kinds of inspired. Here's what I have so far for "Come as You Are." What do you think?

At the foot of the trail, I hit play.

My. Jaw. Drops.

London drags a hand down her chest.

Pops her hip to the left.

To the right.

Lets her head fall back, her hair trailing down her back as she moves to the music.

What do I think?

I think I might come as I am.

I reply.

. . .

Teddy: Change nothing. Not a single fucking thing.

Then I pat myself on the back because I'm so damn focused on this work project with her, and only on the work project.

* * *

Bloom's nuptials are not my first wedding.

I've spun at plenty before tonight. Not as many as I'd like—Edge keeps me pretty busy on the weekends, and those are the prime coupling days. A few months ago, though, I did get to deejay for some friends who were high school sweethearts and got hitched in their early twenties. Late last year I was in charge of the tunes at the reception for a couple of Sam's buddies. My mom also hooked me up with one of her book club friends, who met the love of her life at her twenty-fifth high school reunion, and the sheer number of eighties songs to which they got their groove on made for a helluva night.

What's not to love about being at a wedding? An entire day devoted to celebrating love while surrounded by family and friends? An opportunity to meld two separate worlds into a larger, richer community? Sign me up.

But this is the most fun wedding I've deejayed by far.

Bloom's friends love to dance. They shake and shimmy to every song, with Nate and London busting out the moves. But I haven't seen her for the last hour. Not that I'm clock-watching. Besides, I'm in the zone, lasered in on spinning tunes and only on spinning tunes.

The lady of the evening bounces over to the DJ booth. This is Bloom's first break from the dance floor since she and her hubs cut the cake, and the bride is absolutely glowing.

"Insomnia, you are a certified rock star and an official lifesaver. I've had more compliments on the music than I can count. I'm leaving you the best five-star review in the history of the internet."

"What more can a guy ask for?" Not much. Five-star reviews are up there with blow jobs and tacos. Not always in that order, of course. I've had some pretty righteous tacos.

"Can I pass out a few of these?" Bloom asks, motioning toward a small stack of business cards on the table.

"A few, a lot, all of them—whatever works for you. And thank you. I appreciate it." I shoot her a huge grin, then throw on my headphones to fade to the next track. As a Michael Jackson number shifts into Tina Turner, I sneak a peek and find the other reason why I like this wedding.

Fine, fine.

I've been checking her out all night.

But there's nothing wrong with enjoying the view.

Especially when the brunette beauty heads in my direction.

She walks over to my deejay setup in perfect rhythm to Tina's smoky wailing. God bless tight tops—London's decked out in a light-blue dress with a scoop-neck thing that makes it impossible to look away from her tits, which are bouncing slightly with each step. The dress hits her knees, proper enough for a wedding, but sexy enough to absolutely drive me crazy wondering what she's wearing underneath. Shaking away those thoughts of blue lingerie, white lingerie, red lingerie that matches her glasses—hell, *any* color lingerie—I shoot her a cocky glare. "You just can't stay away from me," I say, heat and challenge in my tone.

"I know. It's impossible. I tried."

"How hard? How hard did you try to stay away?"

"So hard," she teases. "I tried to go on ignoring you for the whole wedding, but I caved just now."

I laugh. "Glad you did. You having fun?"

"I'm having a blast. But I had to duck out for the last hour. Nate and I *both* forgot to bring the wedding gift, so I just ran back to their place to grab it."

"That must've been a really important gift," I say.

She leans in closer and stage-whispers, "It's an Instant Pot." She sets the wrapped cube down on the edge of my table.

"That is important. Some people think the rings make a marriage official . . ."

"But it's actually the Instant Pot," London finishes my joke, and we share a flirty look.

One that spurs me on. "London, why don't you just admit you came to the wedding to see me?"

She narrows her eyes, pointing at my chest. "You crashed the wedding," she teases. "Nate asked me to be his date a week ago."

"If you say so," I toss back.

She crosses her arms. "Just admit you took the job so you could see me."

I laugh. "Fine, fine. I wanted to watch you dance. You caught me."

"Knew it," she says. I shouldn't like flirting with her, because of work, because of my past, because of her brother. But when I'm around London, she has a way of derailing all rational and irrational thought.

I have a way of forgetting everything else.

Like promises I made to myself.

And if I stay in the flirting zone too long, I may lose higher brain function entirely, and I need that for work.

Maybe she's wary of the fine line between flirty and fun too, since she changes the topic to an innocuous one. "So, what's your favorite wedding song ever?"

I go with it, since I'm still on the clock.

"'Uptown Funk' by Bruno Mars has to be a pretty strong contender. That always gets the people moving. But it's also not a wedding without a little 'Unchained Melody.'"

"Mmm, the Righteous Brothers' second-best song."

"True. What would *Top Gun* be, after all, without 'You've Lost That Lovin' Feelin'? But that's probably not the best title for a wedding song."

"Maybe the worst title ever for a wedding song," she says with a laugh. Music is great, but her laughter is quickly becoming my favorite sound. "How about if you had to dance to one song at a wedding? What would it be?"

"What are we talking here? Slow dance? Fast dance? Group dance?"

"Deejay's choice," she says.

"Slow dance definitely goes to 'At Last.' Etta James classic."

"Mmm. And what if you wanted to speed it up a bit?"

"Well, I have a confession to make. I'm an awful fast dancer," I admit sheepishly.

"That's a shame."

"Why's that?"

"I love the fast tunes. If you throw on any Usher or Queen Bey, you can't keep me off the dance floor," she says, tossing her gaze toward the sway of bodies.

But I barely notice the guests, because my head swims with memories of London dancing downtown the other day, and on my phone this morning. I can't stop my eyes from traveling the length of her curvaceous body.

I don't want to stop them on their voyeuristic journey up her legs, around her hips, to the dangerous dip of her dress that exposes just a hint of freckles scattered across the top of her breasts.

"That's definitely something I would love to see, so have at it anytime." I like the idea of dancing with her a lot, so I lean in closer and whisper, "I do kill it at the slow dancing though."

"You don't say?"

"I don't mean to brag, but I was voted best male lead

at cotillion in seventh *and* eighth grade, so . . ." I leave the sentence hanging with a smile.

"In that case, I should probably check out this award-winning slow dancing. For the sake of hypotheses that need to be tested."

"Yes. You should conduct all the experiments. That is, if you insist."

She adopts a serious expression. "I do insist. I need to run my own research. Corruption in the cotillion circuit is well-documented."

I'm about to offer to spin her around on the dance floor for a number when a loud, bright voice hits my ears.

"London!" Bloom exclaims as she makes her way to us, then tugs at London's arm. "My bridesmaids are demanding an epic dancer, and you're an epic dancer. So your presence is requested on the floor."

London's smile takes over her face. "Then we must dance all night long."

Bloom glances my way, then at London, then at me again. Something sparks in her eyes. "But don't you worry. I'll let you return to flirting with this handsome musical Jedi very soon. Come dance."

With a sexy shrug that says she's following the flirting orders from on high, London's eyes travel in my direction.

Exactly where I want them.

I fade into Usher's "Yeah!" and as the beat drops hard and fast, Bloom and London bound to the dance floor to a chorus of cheers from the other guests.

As London dances, her eyes keep meeting mine.

I know exactly what she's thinking.

Same thing I am.

Looks like we both want to break the rogue-kissing pact.

20

Two hours of celebratory revelry later, London is still here with a few lingering guests. The crowd has thinned, and several centerpieces are conspicuously absent. Past a sea of half-empty champagne glasses and partially eaten cake slices, London stands at the edge of the dance floor, fingers toying with her bracelets, looking like the heroine at the end of a wedding sequence in a movie.

Fade in on the candlelight from the tables flickering off her cheeks, the party lights sparkling through her wavy hair. Her soulful brown eyes lock right on me.

She walks over to me. "All right, DJ. Let's test those slow-dancing skills."

"All in the name of science," I say a little huskily because my throat is dry from looking at her. I hit play on "End of the Road." I'm a hopeful guy tonight, and I've had this track ready and waiting for London's invitation. Boyz II Men floats across the warm evening air.

I head in her direction and wrap my arms around

this beautiful woman, bringing her close. Another couple sways together several feet away, but as far as I'm concerned, my whole world begins and ends on this tiny corner of the dance floor, this space where I have zero worries about work and career and a future.

There is no room for anything here but her and me, and how we fit.

"Did Nate leave?" I ask.

"Yes. He went out with some friends."

That answer tells me everything.

She's not leaving with him.

And my body replies—I want her to go home with me.

London leans her head against my shoulder, and I catch a heady whiff of the citrusy scent that makes me dizzy with want. I breathe her in as our bodies come together, drawn closer by this night, this song. The rest of the guests, most long gone now, were drunk on prosecco and gin. I'm intoxicated by this woman.

We don't speak. This moment doesn't need words. With the palm trees rustling from a soft evening breeze and the stage lights mingling with the starlight, we move together, her arms looped around my neck.

Both my hands cup her sculpted ass—because where else would I rest my hands?—and I pull back slightly so I can look at her face. Hard to look anyplace else.

"This must be my lucky day," I say.

"Why's that?" she asks, her eyes all soft and glossy.

"Accidentally booked a dream gig, the event went off without a hitch, and now I'm dancing with a gorgeous, clever, irresistible woman alone on the dance floor."

Furtively, London glances around, tipping her chin to the other couple enjoying the last song of the night. "Technically, we're not alone, Teddy."

"You want to bust me on a technicality? Or should we consider it within the scientific margin of error or whatever you call it?"

"Science and science geeks can only explain so much. Maybe I'm your lucky charm," she whispers against my neck.

Luck. Is this luck? Or is want making me reckless? The club, my relationship with my boss, my burgeoning business—all are at stake.

And yet as I slide my hands up her back, the last thoughts of Archer and my career slink off into the night like the final note of a song fading to silence.

I run my thumb across her cheek in a gentle caress.

She gasps, and with that sexy sound, I give all the way in. I'm not immune to weddings, to slow songs, to flickering strands of lights and warm breezes.

"Maybe you are a good luck charm," I say. "I should call you Lucky."

A grin tugs at her lips. "Did I just get a nickname?"

"Seems you did."

"Better seal it with a kiss."

And because that is the next step of this dance routine, we kiss.

As my lips slide across hers, the moment becomes stronger than me, stronger than my desire to play by the rules and go by the book. Her body melts into mine, and her lips part for me, inviting me in to kiss deeper, harder.

And for longer.

But longer would be better someplace else.

Once our lips separate and we lock eyes, I make a choice.

A dangerous one, but a choice nonetheless.

"About that hypothesis you mentioned last night," I say.

"What about it?" Her question comes out breathy.

"I believe I'd like to take the good-guy challenge."

"Let's take it. Let's take it now."

Looks like we're both ripping up the rogue-kissing pact. Fine by me. The good-guy challenge sounds a helluva lot more satisfying.

London helps with the lights and music breakdown, powered by that same fevered need that's driving me, turned on beyond all reason.

We load all the gear into my car then cruise to my condo, the traffic gods and goddesses gifting us green light after green light.

"I only have thirty minutes," she says in a rush as we get out. "Nate is out for a while, and Mr. Darcy turns into a barking pumpkin at midnight."

"Can he tell time?"

"Yes. Breakfast time, dinnertime, and barking time, which he indulges in if he's alone. Something I learned once when the neighbors complained when we were all out too late."

"Then we better be fast," I say as we bound up the steps.

With supersonic speed, we take Bowie and Vin Scully around the block—I'll answer to Sherri's arched eyebrows tomorrow—then return to my place.

I lock the door, grateful that London still has that hungry look in her eyes.

Pretty sure that look hasn't left mine either.

The energy and fire from the dance floor flicker across her irises. Though it's more of a smolder now.

But that's okay. That gives me the chance to prove good guys have got it going on.

I go for it. Not only for me, but hell—I have the honor of a lot of dudes to defend here.

I finger the hem of her skirt. "So, this window before midnight. I bet we have just enough time to run an experiment."

She taps her chin, playing along. "Gee. What kind of experiment?"

My fingers thread through her hair. "I'd love to prove to you that good guys have what it takes to be great in the bedroom."

She laughs lightly, but her gaze is heated. "What if I don't want to run this test in the bedroom?"

"Living room. Kitchen. Bedroom. A proper experiment requires a variety of controls and variables."

"And testing locations, it seems." She swallows, lifting her chin. "So, what do you have in mind for the next thirty minutes? Or twenty-five, I should say."

I brush featherlight kisses along her neck, making

her shiver as I work my way up to her ear. "Preliminary tests."

"Ohhh," she says, a little shuddery, suggesting she likes where we're going. "But we can do subsequent tests too?" she asks with a hint of sadness in her voice, and I mentally grin at her disappointment that we're not sleeping together tonight.

"We can do all the tests," I say, and I slam my lips to hers, savoring her taste.

We kiss hot and deep for several delicious seconds as I guide her back to the couch, sinking into it, pulling her on top of me. In a practiced move, she takes off her glasses and sets them on the table.

My hands roam over her flat stomach, her back bowing as I touch her. Following her cues, I glide my hands beneath her dress, and in one swift motion, I tug it off, tossing it onto the floor.

There is only one thing to do now—enjoy the view.

I savor every inch of her.

The curves of her tits in her lacy blue bra, the freckles splashed across the valley between them, the soft skin of her stomach. And her legs straddling mine, giving me a fantastic view of matching panties that drive me wild. I press my hard-on against her center, and desire spins wildly through me, racing faster as she grinds down on me.

Our mouths connect again, tongues tangling together. We kiss harder, grinding together in a frenzy, a mad rush to get closer, to touch.

Breaking the kiss, I run my lips over her chest, along the seam of her blue lace bra. Her skin pebbles at my stubbly caress, and she murmurs fantastic words like *yes, more, again*.

What the lady wants . . .

I undo the clasp then slide my hands over the globes of her breasts as her bra slips off. Her tits are . . . words fail me.

Because they are perfect. There's no other way to describe them. A perfect handful with tiny brown nipples that I'm desperate to suck. And I do.

Greedily.

She rewards me with a moan as she throws her head back.

And *holy fuck*.

That move right there makes my skin sizzle.

The way she wants *this*, the way she wants me.

Her nipple hardens in my mouth, making my cock strain tighter against my pants. My hands pay a visit to her ass, squeezing her flesh, all while my lips lavish more attention on her breasts, first one, then the other.

It's only fair.

"You are so fucking sexy, London," I rasp as I come up for air. "These freckles on your chest have been driving me wild all night."

"Seems like fair play. Since you're driving me wild right now."

"Good. Because that's exactly what I want to do to you. You're gorgeous, and I am so unbelievably attracted to you."

"Same. Same for me," she whispers, then lets out a soft, throaty moan before she grinds against my erection. I push up against her, groaning too.

My eyes swing briefly to the wall clock in the kitchen. The countdown is on. "We're at about sixteen minutes before pumpkin dog. That means . . ."

Spinning her around, I lay her back on the couch so she's all stretched out. I lean over her, my lips returning to her neck, nibbling on her ear. She yelps lightly in surprise at the speed of our turn but settles in as I pepper her body with kisses, licks, and sucks.

I trace a line down her front with my tongue, enjoying every inch of her lightly tanned skin, then I slide off the couch so I can kneel on the floor.

This is the only place I want to be on earth—between her legs. I slide my hands up her thighs, delighting at the feel of the soft hairs as I make my way to her hot, wet center.

Face-to-face with her matching blue panties, I trace the lines of her underwear with my finger, a sweet hint of her arousal darkening the middle.

The temperature in me spikes.

There's nothing sexier than the woman you want wanting you right back.

Not a fucking thing in the world.

I hook my finger around the center of her panties and pull toward one thigh, revealing her to me. Soft and glistening with a tuft of hair on her mound, London's pussy shines like a temple, one I am only too happy to worship.

I lick her once, teasing her. And my God, she tastes better than salted caramel. I need access to all of her, want to feast on her, so I guide the lace down her shapely legs, enjoying every inch of her body as I undress her.

As my gaze returns to her center, she parts her legs for me, and my dick thumps harder, my skin heats more. My tongue traces the outline of her pussy, and she gasps then moans low in her throat.

Her sounds urge me on, right up to her clit. I lap gently at first, teasing the pleasure out of her.

As I lick and suck, her body responds with arched hips, hands in my hair, and delicious moans, telling me what's working and what's not. I listen, I adjust, and then I ravage.

I hungrily devour her, and I don't ever want to stop.

But I do like her tits, and judging from the sounds she made earlier when I kissed them, I roll the dice that she'll enjoy double the attention.

My hand flies up her belly, on a fast track for her chest. I cup her breast, massaging and squeezing her nipple as her hips grind against my face.

Yes, I am getting my fill of London right now—my mouth and hands are very happy.

So is she, it seems, as she shouts her approval.

Yes.

So good.

Oh God, oh my God.

Her hands curl tighter around my head, and her moans take on a rhythm of their own as my mouth seeks to match it. I concentrate on her pleasure, driving my face between her legs to the pace she's set.

Her tempo picks up speed.

Her fingers grip me tighter. Hands tug me closer.

"That. Do that. Don't stop," she gasps as I continue my sensual assault. My cock throbs for release, but my focus remains only on her.

Her breathing quickens, and it's time to push her over the edge. I reach for her other breast, squeezing both of them roughly as she grinds against me.

She rocks as I lap at her clit, indulging in every second of her taste, her smell, her pleasure. Soon, her ass is thrusting off the couch. Her thighs grip my head in the best vise grip known to mankind, but even in that position, the *fuuuuckkk* she cries out is unmistakable to my ears.

She freezes in ecstasy for a breath, lets out several wild shudders, and groans.

Best chorus ever.

Slowly, she relaxes into the couch with a happy moan. I gently release her breasts while blowing softly on her core. As her ass hits the leather and she lets out a blissful sigh, I kiss her inner thigh once, twice, and slowly exhale with her. I take a moment to enjoy this charged, wordless silence, the sweet sounds of her satisfaction, her hums and moans. I rise between her legs, gently caressing the tops of her thighs as I sprinkle kisses on her belly.

I make eye contact with her and smile. She grins back, brushes her hair from her face, and exhales deeply. "That was . . ."

Those two words don't even need an adjective.

"Yes, *that was.*"

I head to the kitchen to grab a glass of water, then return and hand it to her.

"Thank you," she says, sitting up straighter on the couch to take a thirsty gulp.

When London sets down her glass, she arches a naughty brow.

Then she asks the best question ever. "Can I do that to you?"

Too bad I can't give her the answer I want to.

21

Her question is an arrow piercing my heart.

Right now I'd choose blow jobs over tacos. Blow jobs over riches. Blow jobs over air.

But I've got a good-guy rep to protect.

The *no* forming on my lips pains me for all of humanity.

It wounds me across the halls of time.

But . . . *dogs*.

"Pretty sure I would love that more than my next breath, but Mr. Darcy needs you. And I won't stand between a dog and his need for after-midnight companionship."

"You *are* a good guy."

I brush my fingers along her arm. "Speaking of, how did I do defending our honor for Emery and Olive?"

She drags her fingers down my chest. "Can I tell them you made me see stars? Supernovas? Galaxies light years away?"

"How about another solar system?"

"All the solar systems," she says, still sounding high on her climax.

And hell, I beam.

Just fucking beam as she gathers her clothes and gets dressed.

I knew great sex would be great fun. And this is officially the most fun I've ever had. Making London's skin flush and her heart pound is everything I imagined great sex would be.

"You have carte blanche to tell them anything about how many constellations you saw. Come to think of it, it would be cruel of you *not* to share it with your girlfriends."

She curls her hand over my shoulder. "Or taunt them with it."

I'd like to thump my chest right now. Stage a half-time show for my prowess tonight.

But I do neither. Instead, I seize this chance.

"We should do it again," I offer. I'm generous like that.

Also, I want her, no matter the risk.

She bites the corner of her lips. Rises onto tiptoe. Brushes a soft kiss against my lips. "Yes."

One perfect word.

She raises a finger. "And I would like to cash that reciprocal rain check very soon."

I give a *no big deal* shrug, even though blow jobs are the deal. "I believe I would be completely amenable to that."

"What do you know? I would too. But right now, I need to take off," she says.

"I'll drive you," I say.

With a grateful smile, she grabs her purse, puts on her glasses, then we leave. I take her home, giving her a quick kiss at the curb, before I return to my place.

Back inside, I'm intensely satisfied.

And also not in the least, considering I've had a raging erection for most of the last hour, and once my eyes swing to the couch and I picture what transpired there moments ago, it returns.

Great.

Fucking dicks.

And this one I'm pretty sure can win the honor of Boner Most Likely To Be Mistaken for a Viagra Overdose.

This au naturel diamond cutter needs some tending to.

I head to the bathroom, shed my clothes, turn on the tap in the shower, and stand under a hot stream of water. I take my aching length in my hand, groaning at the first hint of relief.

This won't take long at all.

I slide my fist up and down my shaft and picture all the things I want to do next with London.

Her scent lingers in my nostrils, drifts through my mind.

I imagine her riding me, and my dick likes that a whole helluva lot.

But my dick has an equal opportunity imagination, so I flip through all the positions I want to try with her —her on top, her reverse cowgirling me, me on top, me on top with her legs draped over my shoulders—oh, yes, that would be fantastic. And how about her on her hands and knees, me pushing her shoulders down so she can raise her ass high in the air?

My senses crackle as I grip harder, stroke faster, a movie reel of all the ways I want to touch her, taste her, have her racing before my eyes.

I want to worship her body with my tongue. Kiss her everywhere. Touch her all over. Slide into her. Feel her clench around me.

Pleasure jolts down my spine, sharp and hot.

My hand shuttles in a blur. Seconds later, I grunt, coming hard, picturing the woman I should stay away from and knowing there's not a chance in hell that I will.

22

The next morning

From the Woman Power Trio, aka the text messages of London and her two besties, Olive and Emery

London: All I'm going to say is you're both wrong. Absolutely incredibly wrong.

Emery: *sits up in bed* *puts glasses on* *perks ears*

Olive: Yes, we want to hear what you've learned about good guys. So please serve up all the salacious details, like the heroine does in a sexy romance novel when she gabs with her besties.

London: Because you love dirty details served in your earbuds.

Olive: Yeah, because earbuds were invented for men with deep, sexy voices to whisper sweet, dirty nothings into. Prove me wrong. Also, since you've heard Dax Long giving it good, then you understand why I go on and on about him.

Emery: After that *kitten, let's have a threesome* clip, yes. Yes, we do. But wait. What's his other name? He goes by the Ostrich, right? Or is it the Rooster? Wait. No. It's the Lizard King!

Olive: *rolls eyes* It's Pegasus. He's the Pegasus.

London: Pegasus, as in the mythical Greek creature?

Olive: He is a man of legend.

London: Hello? Can we discuss real men and real orgasms?

Olive: The Pegasus has given me lots of real orgasms when my hot hubs isn't around. Solo Os are real. Don't be so judgy, you dirty girl. But feel free to make up for it by telling us everything.

London: Let me just say . . . *le sigh*. Le big happy, dirty cloud nine sigh.

Olive: Yay! More, more. Give us more.

Emery: Was it sheet-grabbing, bone-rattling, back-arching good?

London: Let me put it this way. I felt like I had an out-of-body experience when he went down on me.

Olive: So he *is* kind of a Pegasus.

London: It felt quite fantastical. So yes, let's call it a Pegasus-level O. But . . .

Emery: Uh-oh.

Olive: Did he do butt stuff to you, London? *Please say yes. Please say yes.*

London: There was no butt stuff, you pig!

Olive: Oink, oink. So what's the catch?

London: The catch is I like him so much. And I'm pretty sure he really likes me too.

Emery: Liking a man can be hazardous to your health.

London: I know. Trust me, I know.

Emery: What do you like about him?

London: He's funny, clever, kind, and thoughtful. And he listens. He actually listens. So, obviously . . . he's too good to be true.

Olive: Kind *and* thoughtful? He does sound like a book hero. Do you think if your story is made into a romance novel, we could have the Pegasus voice him?

London: Well, he *is* quite magical with his tongue.

Emery: Should we call him the Lizard King, then? And does he have any new tricks we should know about? Not asking for a friend.

London: The trick is this—he was just super into it and so was I.

Emery: *swoons*

Olive: *breaks out emergency nightstand BOB*

Emery: Olive, can you not start diddling yourself while we're texting?

Olive: What made you think I just started?

Emery: You're such a pervert.

Olive: Takes one to know one. And speaking of perverts, I want to hear from pervy London. Tell us more about the Lizard King's magic tongue.

London: Honestly, I think he just wanted me to feel really good. That was the magic.

Olive: You are so far gone. Also, that's kind of how it should be. But you've probably forgotten because it's been such a long time. I think you might be suffering from sex amnesia.

London: That comes after the sex drought, right?

Emery: But it ends with the sex feast. Are you having a sex feast?

London: I would like to be. I kind of can't stop thinking about him. What the hell am I supposed to do?

Emery: Only one thing *to* do. Emergency meeting to discuss. Because it sounds like it's way more than just sex.

London: I think it's been more than just sex from the first day I met him. He never seemed like a "just sex" guy. Is that good or bad?

Olive: Let me be serious for one hot second. It's good. It's also dangerous.

London: Ugh. That's my worry. He's made it kind of clear that he's not really interested in anything more. Because of working for my brother and all that.

Emery: Your brother is hot.

London: Wow. On that note, my lady boner is gone.

Olive: Mine's not. Archer is a babe.

London: You're married!

Olive: Married. Not dead.

Emery: But on a more serious note, are you going to say something to Archer?

London: Not yet. But if something came of it? Yeah, I would. I don't like lying to him.

Olive: Sweets, you're not lying to him. You're just not telling him till there is something to tell.

London: True. I guess we will see if anything happens.

Olive: I bet it does. And in the meantime, if the Pegasus plays the Lizard King with the magic tongue in the audiobook of your love life, here's a great primer on dirty talk. I listened to this the other night, and then texted Hawke to be good and ready when he got home. I'm going to send you a snippet of *All Night with the Inked Biker Next Door*, read by Dax Long, aka the Pegasus.

"I'm going to give it to you and give it to you hard. That's the only thing I want on earth. To make you feel so fucking good."

London: Sorry, I didn't hear you. I was busy with my BOB.

Olive: Knew it. Called it.

23

As I finish up a long walk with Bowie, a text message pings on my phone.

Like a trained circus monkey, my dick stands at attention.

Hopeful fucker.

But not without cause—the message is from London.

London: I did as promised.

Teddy: Told your friends?

London: Yes.

Teddy: And?

London: Olive sent me a naughty audiobook full of dirty talk, and I . . . well, did I mention you give good dirty talk?

Teddy: Is this another good-guy hurdle?

London: It is. Also, I just learned I really like dirty talk. Can I order up some more for the next time I see you?

Teddy: Your order will be served HOT.

London: Teddy?

Teddy: London?

London: I know you said that this can't really be anything, and I get that. I respect that. But I really want to see you again.

Teddy: Same. I want the same.

London: Are we still on for the radio station?

Teddy: On like Donkey Kong.

Bowie and I bound up the steps to my condo and head inside. He laps some water in the kitchen as I flop down on the couch in a text message haze, happy and dizzy. My phone pings again.

With a dopey smile, I slide my thumb across the screen.

And freeze.

.   .   .

Archer: How's everything going with the dance routines? The partners are excited to see what you and London are working on.

Guilt wraps its prickly fingers around me. Digs into my chest. Winds down my spine. Talk about the worst timing ever.

Teddy: I'm going to see her tonight at the radio station. We'll work hard on that set list.

Archer: Working hard. That's what I like to hear.

I wince.

Why did I say *work hard*?

I squeeze my eyes shut, wishing away the guilt, trying to kick it under the table.

* * *

A little later, I call Sam, and we hit the tennis courts for a game. I focus entirely on beating the fuck out of him in straight sets so that I don't think at all about how I'm lying to my boss.

But the truth is, all I can focus on is London the woman.

Only the woman.

Apparently, that means I can't annihilate Sam, since the fucker pulls off a rare victory.

"I rule!" He thrusts his arms in the air when he finishes me off, racket in one hand.

"Good game," I say.

"Epic." He hands me a towel as we walk over to our bags. "But you were out of your element, bro. I can read your energy, and it's all out of whack."

"That's your official diagnosis? Out of whack?"

"That's as official as it gets from Yogi Sam, Assessor of Energy. What's the story? Was the wedding gig full of bad mojo?"

I scoff, because that's the furthest thing from the truth. "The wedding was great. London was there."

"And?" he asks, waiting for me to fill in the gap.

"And she came home with me." I offer it like the confession it is.

"Ohhhhh." The drawn-out syllable sounds like a warning. "So what's next?" he asks as we reach my car. "How are you going to deal with that?"

By seeing her again.

Only, that's not the *right* answer.

But it's the choice I'm making.

"I'm seeing her tonight."

He lets out a low whistle then claps my shoulder. "I'm not going to tell you what to do or what not to do. All I will say is this—be careful, bro. Can't always see the riptides until it's too late."

It's great advice, but I'm not sure I'm going to follow it. When it comes to London, I'm already swimming out way too far.

24

My father whacks another softball to the end of the batting cage.

"You go, stud."

That's my mom, encouraging her man. It's awesome. Not weird, just awesome.

Well, I could do without the *stud* bit.

"Impressed, son?" my dad asks, glancing my way.

"I'm always impressed with your softball prowess."

He digs in at the plate, eyeing the red pitching machine. "You should come to my games, then. Cheer me on."

My jaw drops. "I was there the other week. Did you not recognize your only son at the game, yelling from the bleachers?"

He slams the ball. "Oh, that's right—that was you. Didn't realize you were there, since you yell like an ant."

"An ant?" I shoot back, puzzled, as he cracks another ball all the way to the fencing.

My mother tsks me. "Yes, sweetheart, don't you

know? You have to cheer incredibly loud for your father. He needs a lot of praise at his age."

My dad gives her a smile. "I've needed a lot of praise at every age."

"Duly noted," I say. "So we've reached the stage in our relationship where I'm now the parent and you're the millennials yearning for participation trophies?"

My dad seems to consider this, then nods. "Sounds about right."

Another ball arcs toward Dad, but this time he over-swings and it's a rare miss. We both laugh, and he takes a deep breath and settles back into the box.

After a few more cuts, we finish and pack up, heading to the café next to the cages, my parents holding hands as we walk. We order lunch, then my mom sets her hands on the table. "How was the wedding? I want to hear all about it."

"The bride was incredibly happy. I checked this morning on Yelp, and she already left me a five-star review, which was definitely not something I thought she'd take care of on her wedding night, but hey, she did," I say, spreading my napkin on my lap. "Plus, I've already had one person reach out to me after seeing the review, asking to book me for an upcoming gig."

Dad pumps a fist. "This is good. This is exactly what you've been wanting. You've been a little lost for the last year."

That's my dad—not one to mince words. "True. And I think this is going to help me focus on growing my new business, building it from the ground up. I won't be distracted now."

But that's not entirely honest. When I got home from tennis and got in the shower, I was 100 percent focused on London again.

My dad gives me a warm grin. "It's good to see you moving on after Tracy. You were in a funk for a while after things fell apart with her."

"And that's understandable," my mom weighs in. "But speaking of moving on from Tracy . . ." She trails off in that inviting sort of tone that warns the next question is coming in three, two, one . . . "Have you met anybody else?"

"Since you asked me a few days ago?" I counter, deflecting.

She nods earnestly. "Yes, love can happen quickly." She snaps her fingers. "Just like that."

This is the moment of truth. I like my parents. I've been pretty open with them my entire life. I told them when I had my first kiss my freshman year of high school. I told them about the girl I took to senior prom. I've discussed sex with them. They bought me my first box of condoms and took me out for pizza after my first breakup. They raised me in a household without any shame.

They kissed in front of my sister and me. They went out together and made it clear that date nights were important for a couple.

They've always talked openly about intimacy and the power of love. I've always believed in love because of them.

A part of me desperately wants to continue down that path of truth and say, *Yes, I'm seeing this awesome woman.*

But am I seeing her? Are we dating?

No, you dumbass, you're not fucking dating; you're messing around with her. She's your boss's little sister, and you're hooking up with her on the side, which feels entirely wrong.

And entirely what I can't say to my parents.

"There's not really anyone," I say with a smile and a shrug.

And as our food arrives, I feel shitty about lying.

But not so shitty that it stops me from seeing London that night.

25

That evening, I settle into one of my happy places—behind the soundboard at the public radio station, putting tracks together for my Monday night show.

I'm trying to keep my mind focused on my work project with London, but if my set list tonight is any indication, my brain is not cooperating. The show is packed with soulful R & B. Seems that some part of me thinks this work meeting is a good excuse to chill to some vocalists who know how to tell a woman how they feel.

And Al Green can do just that.

Should I follow his lead? Tell London I'm a little crazy for her?

Wait.

What the . . .?

Snap out of it.

I am *not* feeling Al Green levels of hearts fluttering over my head.

Nope. Just enjoying some tunes. That's all. Like

William Bell. I switch to him next, then lean back in the chair and enjoy the song along with my listeners.

I turn my mic on as the track fades out. "And now, because music, like sex, is better with a partner, here's Marvin Gaye and Tammi Terrell singing 'Ain't No Mountain High Enough.'"

When the song ends, it's one minute to ten. Time to wrap up.

"I hope you've enjoyed this week's wind down, and whether you're in the mood tonight for some 'Love and Happiness' or just looking to 'Get It On,' I hope you find someone to share it with. This is DJ Insomnia, reminding you that you can sleep when you're dead. Peace."

The "On Air" light flicks off as I cut the feed, energized by the post-show buzz.

Or is tonight's high courtesy of anticipation? London will be here any second, and we'll be alone.

The engineer took off already, since I'm used to locking up, and my show's the last of the night.

In the quiet of the studio, I have my laptop open to cue up the "Come as You Are" remix I made for London's revue, when she texts that she's downstairs. I buzz her into the building. "Third floor. End of the hall. There may or may not be ice cream."

"Do not tease about ice cream."

"Fine. There is sadly no ice cream." I wish now that there were. "But I can't wait to tease you about other things."

A minute later, the door to the studio control room opens, and London breezes in. "Your music partner has arrived," she says with a flourish, and tosses her bag onto the couch.

Partner. Did she listen to my show? Hear my comment about duets? If so, that's hella hot. "Music is better with a partner," I say, and the glint in her eyes behind those cute red glasses is my answer.

I drink her in, from her flowy floral top that has the good sense to hug her breasts, to the curve of her hips in her snug jeans. My jeans become a bit snugger too. A lot snugger, actually.

"It's good to see you." I try to keep the mood casual as I stand, cross the studio, and wrap her in a quick hug.

We separate as she checks out the room, taking in the posters advertising bands at the Hollywood Bowl and the Greek. "This place is exactly how I pictured it. I have to confess, I was hoping I'd feel like I was in a Nick Hornby novel," she says.

"It's *High Fidelity* in radio station form."

"Exactly. Epic show posters, a few gold records."

I gesture to the couch. "Make yourself comfortable." As she sinks into the cushions, I take a seat opposite her at the desk so I can man the controls. As I settle in, her gaze lingers briefly on my stomach and the bulge in my pants. The hungry look in her eyes only sends more blood rushing to the region. Last night's oral offer has been running through my mind continually. How can I be expected to get any playlist-planning done when she's eye-fucking me like that?

It's an impossible feat. Eye-fucking wins, fair and square.

She rubs her palms, at the ready. "What have you got for me?"

Oh, I have plenty for you, London.

I click on the mix, launching into the opening notes of Nirvana.

"You said you wanted something playful, fun, and also iconic. And when you busted out those moves downtown, then again in that video, I kept thinking about the type of music that women love, that gets them to grab their friend's hand and say, 'Oh my God, I love this song.' But I also thought about how some things make us hear a song a new way. So . . ." I stretch out the word as I build to my big idea. "I've put some mash-ups together that combine rock edginess with pop effervescence. Something like this." I switch from the Cobain track to the start of an Imagine Dragons tune.

Her eyes light up. "I love them. My friends do too."

Yup. Called it. "Let's give the audience what they want."

"Brilliant."

The second the lyrics are set to kick in, Taylor Swift launches into "Shake It Off."

London's eyes spark, and my chest tightens with a growing hope. I want her to like this way more than I expected.

She seems into it, but not quite sold, until I move on to the next tune—a Duran Duran number that the ladies at Edge always seem to sing their own karaoke to, "Hungry Like the Wolf."

Something like glee crosses her face.

Pride suffuses me. Nothing beats impressing the woman you like.

Except sex.

That's better.

But this is pretty damn close.

As Survivor's "Eye of the Tiger" blends in with the chorus, London picks up her imaginary Strat and strums the air.

"You've been practicing. I can tell," I say of her air-shredding.

"I've got a competition to enter, remember? And apparently I'll have to learn animal hybrid tunes . . . because did you really just combine wolf and tiger songs?"

"I'm not afraid to go carnal," I say, and her mouth forms a sexy O as she sets down her imaginary guitar and pick when Survivor hits the chorus. London bobs her head, visualizing her choreography, I suspect.

"I have a verdict," she says, and I can't tell from her tone if she's deep in thought or deeply disappointed. She relieves me with her next words. "I love it, Teddy. It's exactly what I'm looking for. The pop lyrics are familiar enough to get a club pumped up, but the rock jamming underneath makes it a totally unique sound. You're soooo good."

My body tingles at her words. I could listen to her compliment me all night long. And hell, I'd like to earn praise from her, in all different ways.

She mentions other artists she wants to hear, like P!nk and Ed Sheeran, so I make some notes to work on it and send her another round tomorrow.

We listen to a few other tunes I have cued up, soaking in the surround-sound vibe of the speakers, the way music bathes the studio. Archer's right—it does feel like the club in here.

When we've made real progress, I declare our work done for the evening and head to the mini-fridge, grabbing two cans of seltzer and handing her one. "Celebratory toast?"

After we pop them open, we clink aluminum and say, "Cheers." I slide next to her on the couch.

"That *was* hard work," she says. "You do seem like you need a break."

"Hey, it's been a long day," I say, a hint of fatigue coming through. "Tennis with Sam, lunch with my parents, radio show, thinking about the situation with you all day." I probably shouldn't admit that last bit, but when I'm next to her like this, the truth wants to come out.

"Ah, yes. It *is* a situation."

"It didn't help either when my mom asked if I was seeing anyone." The guilt and confusion from lunch comes rushing back, like a sharp, stabbing pain.

She takes a sip of her bubbles, her brow knitting, like she's mulling this over. "And what did you say?"

"Honestly? I lied. Or at least I kinda didn't answer. And I don't know why exactly. Because I love my folks and I've always been up-front with them about my relationships, and I wanted to tell them about you. But I don't know . . ." I trail off, not sure exactly what I'm trying to say. Not sure where we should go from here.

How to be careful and also be present tonight. Or if I can.

"But this isn't a relationship." It comes out a little sad, and that note in her voice stops me for a moment.

But then, I can't argue with her.

It's not.

I'm the one who made it clear that we couldn't have one.

I laid down the law.

"Right," I say, a little heavily. "For all the reasons we talked about."

"Exactly," she says, adjusting her tone, speaking brightly now. Maybe too brightly? Hard to say, but I swear for a second it sounds like she's convincing herself.

Like maybe she wishes we could have something more.

Or is that wishful thinking on my part?

Likely so, and with that in mind, I let the next words make landfall. "Except we aren't going to be working together that long . . ."

It sounds like an invitation, one that spells out how I'm potentially up for more in the future.

Trouble is, even though she won't be working for the club much longer, she'll always be my boss's sister.

And I don't want to mix business with pleasure.

Especially since leaving the club isn't an option.

My deejay business has barely gotten off the ground. It's like a hot-air balloon floating a few feet above earth, sandbags still very much attached.

"That's true," she says, perched on the edge of the couch like she's waiting for me to say more.

But, *fuuuuck*, I can't say what I want to say. Can't do what I want to do.

I can say *this* much though.

"You've got to know, if I didn't work for your brother, this would be different," I say, gesturing from her to me and back. "It would. I swear."

Her smile curves wickedly. "Good to hear."

"But I do work for him. And more than that, I just can't make the same mistakes I made last time. Everything was tangled up with Tracy's dad, and when I got out of that relationship, I had to start over. Rebuild from scratch."

"I don't want you to be in that position. You need to know I don't want to get in the way of your career. That's the last thing I want."

Damn. Why does she have to be so understanding? Oh right, because she's awesome. Thanks, universe, for dangling a fantastic woman in my path—a woman *I can't have*.

"And I *need* the job. I need the raise I'm up for too, since it'll help me with my own business." I emphasize the word *need* because, well, it deserves emphasis. "My event business isn't ready to fly on its own just now. Maybe someday. But not yet. So I need to keep building that. I said as much to Sam when I told him about you."

"You told your friend about me?" Her tone pitches up like she's intrigued, maybe delighted, by this fact.

"Hell, yeah. Told him what an incredible first date we had. He's wise beyond his years. Honestly, he keeps me more centered than he probably knows. He's a good dude."

"Sounds like my Olive. She and Emery are my rocks —my diamonds really. We all went to college together, and I'm so happy they both live here. They've made settling in LA so much easier for me."

"Here's to friends." I lift my can to hers.

"Not for the many, but for the true."

"I like that," I say, then take a drink.

"Thanks," she says. "Although, I can hear Olive whispering in my ear right now telling me friendships aren't everything. Friendships are there so you have someone to talk to about your awesome sex life, she'd say."

"So *is* it? Awesome?"

Her eyes glint. "It's been showing real promise recently. I met this adorable guy," she says, using the same word she did on our sushi date.

"I hear adorable is actually quite sexy."

"You heard correctly." This conversation has taken a welcome turn away from Shouldn't City and toward Why Notsville. Her voice is pure sex, and her eyes are smoldering. I set my can on the table, and she does the same.

"You know what else I heard?" I ask playfully.

"What's that?"

"Adorable guys are great kissers. It can be proven in the adorable-guy challenge."

"Challenge accepted. Lay it on me."

"With pleasure." I lean in, gently remove her glasses, set them on the coffee table, and steal one long kiss, claiming her mouth, savoring the taste of her.

My head swims with desire, and I let out a low groan. She pulls back, eyes hazy. "I think you're right. About us focusing on the job."

"Right," I say, deflated, even though her eyes haven't lost any of that fire.

"But I think we're probably okay to focus on different kinds of jobs. Like, say, blow . . . jobs." She gives a hint of separation between those last two words, and it's one of the sexiest things I've ever heard.

"That sounds like a great job to focus on," I rasp as she inches closer to me and lays her hand on my stomach.

She slides her fingers between the buttons of my shirt, teasing my abs. I curl a hand around the back of her head, drawing her to my mouth. Losing myself in London. Giving in to this moment that feels so right. *She* feels right. And I want that. I want more of her.

She takes over the kiss, flicking her tongue over my lips while she unbuttons my shirt, caressing my chest. Part of me wants to stop her—it's after hours, but someone still might come into the studio. But she seems into it, and hey, it's just a shirt.

"Mmm. Nice chest. Nice pecs. Nice everything," she whispers in my ear as she parts the material, dips her head, and presses a kiss to my chest. I shudder from her touch, running my fingers through her hair as she feathers kisses on my pecs and nipples. Her soft lips on my skin send shock waves rushing through my body. My cock throbs in my pants as she scrapes her fingernails down my abs.

Then, in one smooth motion, she unclasps the

button at my fly and tugs at my zipper. She slides effortlessly off the couch so she's on her knees in front of me, just as I was for her last night. She's a sensual goddess, a lustful contradiction. Submissive on her knees, but powerful in her eyes, the desire to please me shining in those irises. Part of me wants to toss her on her back and fuck her so we can experience that pleasure together, but something else tells me to relax, to enjoy this.

Her hand plays with the waistband of my boxer briefs, and her eyes dart to the door. She seems aware of the distant possibility of us being found like this, and instead of pulling my pants down, she reaches inside and grabs my length. The feel of her soft hand on me for the first time draws out a groan from deep within.

An appreciative smirk plays on her face as she runs her hand down my shaft to cup my balls, freeing me from my boxers, exposing all of me to her. She licks her lips as her eyes focus on my dick, and I swear I almost come from the look on her face alone.

"This is a pretty nice cock too," she says.

"Nice?" I tease.

Taking her time, she whispers in a voice like smoke, "Incredible."

If I thought I was going to blow from the heat in her eyes, her dirty words have me at the edge of desire. With her hands on my thighs, she drags her soft tongue up my length, teasing me from balls to tip. She plants firm, sucking kisses down the throbbing vein as her hand grips the base. Her lips and her touch have my cock jumping against my stomach.

"Now that's incredible," I murmur, as she pumps up the length of my shaft, stopping to thumb the pre-come off the tip. She brings it to her lips, her eyes going hazy as she licks off the taste of me.

I heat up as I get to know London's deliciously dirty side, fire sparking across every inch of my body.

Her hand smooths down my dick until she's cupping my balls, driving me crazy with her teasing touch.

I let out a low growl that sounds like a warning. I'm dying for her to take me in her mouth, but London has other plans—plans to make me beg, it seems.

Her mouth travels the length of my shaft as her eyes stay locked on mine.

"Your mouth is amazing," I grind out as her tongue reaches the tip and she swallows the head of my dick in one decadent motion.

A motion that sends lightning racing up my spine.

She takes her time, exploring my dick with her lips. And I'm all too happy for her to get to know my favorite body part.

As she sucks the head, her tongue laves my dick in an intoxicating swirl.

I'm not above pleading.

Hell, just now I'd beg, borrow, and steal for her to swallow me whole. When I groan so loudly that I wonder if the engineer who left long ago can hear, she takes mercy and, at last, at long fucking fast, goes deeper, moaning around me.

Her murmurs, those sexy, dirty sounds, shoot pinpricks of pleasure through my body.

I lay my head back against the cushions, savoring

her magnificent touch. "Your mouth . . . so good," I croak before my mind can no longer form any thoughts, overcome by the buzz of pleasure, by the promise of blissful torment.

She sets a languid rhythm, taking her time, traveling the length of my cock, her lips and hand moving together. On the next stroke, her mouth relaxes, and she takes more.

Her hand travels lower, massaging my balls, as her lips draw me impossibly deeper in her throat. That sensation of her mouth full of me has my thighs crackling with energy, my head swimming with desire. She is intoxicating, and I'm high on her and ready to explode.

"Gonna come," I grunt. She sucks harder, squeezes my balls just a little tighter, and lets out one more delicious moan.

My cock pulses inside her mouth, the first wave of euphoria crashing into me. As my hips thrust, my orgasm overtakes me, and a series of pulsing spasms shoots the length of my body. The release gives way to a floating sensation as I glide on a cloud of pleasure.

She slows her movements and swallows in flawless rhythm with my body.

We spend a few moments suspended in this blissed-out state. As I come down from my high, she lets go of me with one final mind-blowing lick.

Our eyes lock.

"Un. Fucking. Real," I mutter, trying to catch my breath.

"Mmm. I'm glad you liked."

"Oh, I liked. I fucking loved. Jesus, that was . . ." And I finish the thought by sighing happily.

She rocks back on the floor, but I grab her arm gently and pull her up to me, making room for her to nestle into my chest on the couch. She rests her head against me as I wrap an arm around her and kiss her hair.

"That's got to be the best work meeting I've ever been a part of," I offer, as real-world thoughts return to my mind—most of them working out ways to reconcile the sex we want to have with the relationship we need to avoid.

26

Sure, I have theories. About fate, about luck, about great sex.

But never once did I speculate that an excellent sexual encounter would sate me.

Not once did I dream of thinking, *That'll be enough.*

But what I didn't anticipate was how, despite feeling so satisfied, I could want her so insanely much again.

Like, immediately.

Maybe, say, right now.

Well, okay, after I recover. But that's simply a matter of time, not will.

I hope, though, that she wants all the same things I do.

More connection, more closeness, more of this night that feels like an escape. That feels like it exists out of the calendar, out of time.

After I pull up my boxer briefs and zip my jeans, I run a hand along her hair. "What the hell are we going to do next?"

It's as much a rhetorical question as a practical one.

She tap-dances her fingers down my chest. "I have some ideas."

I wiggle my brow. "I bet your ideas would like my ideas."

"Do your ideas involve both of us getting naked?"

I groan. My dick is going to be showing off for her again. Soon. "Yes, they do. But the big question is, can we really do this?"

Her expression goes serious too. "I don't want the night to end. I heard what you said earlier. I get it. This is what it is. But I like this too much to put any brakes on."

"I'm afraid somebody may have cut my brakes when it comes to you," I say, then I brush a kiss along her cheek. "And I mean that in every way. Not just the physical. You know that, right?"

Her lips curve into a soft grin. "I think I do know that."

I squeeze her hand. "I mean it. I meant everything I said earlier. But I mean this too. Being with you is one of the easiest things I've ever done, not just in ages, but ever. Talking to you, laughing with you—everything with you. It's kind of crazy."

"It's kind of crazy good."

"Kind of wild that twenty minutes ago, I was telling you that things would be different if I had a different job and how I don't want to repeat the mistakes of the past . . . and now all I want is to spend more time with you."

Her smile is sweet and sexy. "I guess the blow job worked, then."

I don't return the joke. Instead, I tuck her hair behind her ear. "No. It's not the blow job. Though it was spectacular. It's you. Just you. Nothing about this feels like a mistake."

"I know," she whispers softly. "I feel the same."

I press my forehead to hers, my hand brushing over her soft hair. I'm savoring this moment. It feels like we're teetering on the edge. Of saying more. Of admitting hearts and feelings and all those other things.

But the last twenty-four hours with her have simply been a bubble, and I'd do well to remember that.

We separate, and I do up the buttons on my shirt. "I want to taste you, touch you, feel you. Slide inside you. Watch you melt. Make you come a second time and then do it again," I say. "Which we really shouldn't do in here."

She laughs, breathes out hard, then waves a hand in front of her face. "Okay, you make me laugh and you turn me on at the same time. Is that your special skill?"

"Why, yes, it is."

"But the trouble is . . ."

"Barking pumpkin dog."

"Nailed it," she says a little sadly.

"Well, if we were dating, what would you do?"

"If we were dating?" She asks the words as if she's tasting them. As if they're cherries or ice cream and she likes the way they feel on her tongue.

Hell, I like the way they *sound* on her tongue.

"I think we'd go to my house," she continues, "pick him up, and take him to yours."

"So that's what we'd do if we were dating?"

"Yes."

"Then we'll do that."

And it feels like we are dating. This is a dating conversation. This is a few days with a woman I'm falling for. These are the type of days I'll remember two, three, four years down the road when we talk about how the two of us started to fall for each other.

Or maybe I'm getting ahead of myself.

"The very puppy-friendly pooch Sir David Bowie and I extend a most humble invitation to Mr. Darcy for an evening in our home," I say in an over-the-top British accent. "Would you like to bring Mr. Darcy to my house?"

"Mr. Darcy accepts your invitation. However, he is a horn dog."

"He will be in excellent company, then."

* * *

A little later, London pulls up at my house in her cherry-red VW bug. She parks the car, unbuckles her dog, and steps out with Mr. Darcy in her arms.

Little dude wags his tail when he sees me waiting with Bowie, so I scratch the small pooch's chin, then give him a kiss on the head.

She sets him on the ground, and the dogs greet each other.

I waggle the dog bags in my hand. "I got the dog bags. Please try not to get too excited."

"Oh, that is so sexy," she says.

I take her hand and we walk our dogs and they do their business. It's not romantic, yet it's ridiculously romantic because the stars are out, the night air is cool, and we're wandering through my neighborhood like we would if we were dating.

If we were together.

Everything about tonight feels like it could be repeated for the next week and the next month and the next year. Everything about this feels like this could be how we are.

I squeeze her hand.

She smiles in my direction. "What's that for?"

I shrug. "Nothing. Everything. I don't know."

She laughs too. "I feel the same way." She nudges my elbow as we round the corner on my street. "Hey, on a scale of one to ten, how great have the last twenty-four hours been?"

"Five hundred," I say.

"C'mon. I was thinking a thousand."

"We haven't even had sex yet. Let's wait for the sex till we give it a thousand."

"That's my point. It's amazing with you even if we don't sleep together."

I groan—a groan of happiness. I stop in my tracks, my dog by my side, her dog by her side, and I cup her cheek. "You're right. It's a thousand already." I press a kiss to her lips. When we separate, I say, "I like hanging out with you. I liked it last night, and I liked it today. I like working together. I like all the things."

"What do you know? I like all the things too. It's all pretty damn good." Her tone goes wistful again. There's a note of sadness that makes me feel like a jackass. What the hell am I doing? I know this can't go anywhere. Not anywhere I want it to.

But I'm doing it anyway.

I sidestep the *us* and focus on something that I can say with absolute certainty. "By the way, I think your dance is going to be incredible. You're going to nail that portfolio, and you're going to do great things at the club."

"Thanks. I'm pretty happy with it. I think we created a cool thing together. I'm going to put the finishing touches on it tomorrow. Also, you're a pretty good deejay. I'm sure your new business will boom."

"I'm nowhere near ready yet to go out on my own. But someday."

I tell myself the same could apply to her and me. Maybe someday.

Maybe someday when things change at the job.

Maybe someday when I sort out what I'm doing.

Maybe someday when I get a better handle on things and figure out my life. Maybe then I'll be able to have that maybe-someday with her.

But for now, I'm going to relish tonight for all that it is.

As we return to my building and head upstairs, I adopt a TV informercial voice. "Have you ever considered how amazing the hedgie toy is?"

"As in the greatest dog toy ever invented?"

"It is indeed the best toy in the history of dog toys. Whoever invented it deserves an award."

"All the awards," she says as I open the door to my condo, and we unsnap our dogs' leashes.

I toss a hedgie to Bowie and another to Mr. Darcy. They take them to opposite ends of the living room. As they focus on the utter amazingness of their toys, I take London to my bedroom, she removes her glasses, and we undress each other.

None of this feels like we're messing around. None of it feels like we're hooking up. None of this feels like it's going to end soon.

All of it feels like we're just starting.

Here we are.

In my bedroom.

Stripped bare.

Ready.

Her eyes glimmer with desire as we lunge at each other. I tug her onto the bed, on top of me. Our bodies crash together, and the feel of skin on skin makes my head hazy.

She moans, low and throaty. I thread my hands in her hair, bringing her mouth to mine.

We kiss, needy and hungry—the kind of kiss that's both desperate and a prelude. A kiss that won't last long, because we both need more.

More than kissing. More than mouths.

We need connection.

Hell, I crave it.

We kiss recklessly, unchained. Our mouths saying words that extend beyond *maybe someday*.

I grab a handful of her hair, pulling her head back

roughly, and slam my lips to hers. I'm kissing her everywhere, devouring her, consuming her. Her lips, her cheeks, her chin, neck, and ear.

She tastes like heaven as her tongue tangos with mine. My hands glide down her smooth back, clasping her ass—her gorgeous, fantastic ass that I want to spank, bite, kiss. I squeeze her flesh, letting her know with my touch how much I want her.

With a soft but sexy laugh, she pulls away from my mouth. "You trying to tell me you like my ass?"

I give her a salacious grin. *"Love.* I love your ass. It's spectacular."

She slides her hand around to mine, kneading it too. "Back at you," she says, then returns to my lips.

The press of her body against mine is incredible, but I want her under me. I flip her onto her back, then admire the view. Her lithe, lovely body. Her soft stomach. Her perky tits.

Right here for me to adore.

I bury my face between her breasts, sucking and licking feverishly while she cries out.

"Yes. Mmm. Love that."

I love her mouth, her words, the way she talks back.

It's fucking fantastic to be with a woman who tells you what she likes. Who's unafraid to voice her desires, to ask for what she wants.

Her body's damn good at communicating too. She's rocking her hips, arching her back, making it clear she wants more.

After I worship at the altar of her breasts, I pull back, rise up, and take her in.

This is all I want. To be naked with London. To be here with her.

She runs her fingers along my chest, then trails them down my arms with wild arousal in her eyes. Her fingernails dig gently into my flesh, sending shivers of pure bliss coursing through my body.

When she reaches the tattoo on my left arm, her breath hitches and her eyes glaze.

"I finally get to see the tattoo," she purrs playfully.

"I knew you could convince me."

"What does it mean to you? Why did you have it done?"

"It's a Celtic trinity knot. Body, mind, spirit," I say, guiding her hand over each point. "A reminder to stay in balance. Though the 'body' part is kinda dominating right now."

"That is—" she begins, but I don't let her finish. I kiss her again, hard, taking her lower lip between my teeth.

My cock throbs, my chest heats, and I've never known arousal like this before.

I move off her, wedge myself next to her, and slide a hand between her legs as I seek out her heat. My fingers glide over her pussy, and she gasps, bows her back, and whispers, "Will you fuck me with your fingers first?"

Will I?

More like *Can I please do everything filthy and beautiful to you all night long?*

But words aren't easy to form with desire pulsing hard and fast in my body, taking over my mind.

I don't need many though.

Just one.

"Yes."

I run my fingers over her wetness, centering on her clit, seeking her pleasure. Her body responds to my touch but seems to beg for more too.

I give it to her as I slide a finger inside her, and she lets out the most delicious moan I've ever heard.

I add another finger, and she rocks into my hand as I press my palm to her swollen clit. She shakes, moaning words that urge me on as I touch her.

So good.

Yes.

God, yes.

She's close, so damn close. I massage and rub as she grinds against my hand, my fingers, my palm.

Her legs tighten, and she cries out.

She doesn't stop.

Her moans and groans echo through the air. I stroke her through her climax, slowing down as her noises ebb.

Then, gently I remove my hand, reach for a condom from the nightstand, and suit up. Her eyes are glossy, brimming with satisfaction as she watches me roll it on.

"I want you so much," she murmurs.

"You have no idea how much I want you," I whisper.

"I think I might," she says, and I lower myself on top of her, rubbing the head of my cock over her glistening pussy.

She reaches a hand down, grabs the base of my cock, and guides me into her.

My eyes fall shut at the first intoxicating feel of her

heat gripping me. I sink deeper, shuddering as her body takes me.

When I sink deeper still, we both tremble then groan at the same time.

This feels so fucking good.

"*You*," I rasp.

But I don't say anything more.

Because I am consumed with the electric intensity of being inside the woman I want.

"Yes," she moans as I rock in and out to the rhythm of her moans and the pressure of her hands on my ass.

We're fast at first, going hard and deep and desperate.

But soon, we slow. We take our time, enjoying each other, exploring the limits of our pleasure. I grind deep inside her, wanting to prolong the moment, the night. I lower myself to my forearms, getting closer, my chest against hers. She wraps her legs tighter around me, bringing me deeper too.

Burying my face in her neck, I inhale oranges, getting high off it. Her scent drives me wild, makes me thrust harder.

She moans, arching her back, liking this new speed.

"Don't stop," she whispers.

"No plans to."

Her legs begin to quake. She's close again. I am too, but I continue to savor each thrust.

With her fingernails digging into my back, she grips me harder, a plea for me to pick up the pace even more. I'm only too happy to oblige. I pump faster and harder, listening to the sounds of her moans, learning the language of her body.

One more drive into her, and she shakes and clenches, calling out a delirious *oh God, yes, oh my fucking God.*

Once her thighs lock and an orgasm overtakes her, my body follows hers into oblivion as I push impossibly deeper into her and explode.

For a moment, there is only stillness.

My body is taut, my mind calm, and I am bliss.

We inhale each other, and I relax against her tight body.

Slowly, I roll off of her, and she lets out a soft whimper.

Quickly, I take off the condom, toss it in a trash can in the bathroom, and return to her with a warm washcloth.

She's still lying there, content, melting into the bed.

Already missing her contact, I join her. She takes the washcloth from me as I trail my hand across her sweat-glistened body to her inner thigh. Reluctantly, we come back to earth together, and I toss the washcloth into the hamper.

She sighs contentedly as my fingers trail along the goose bumps that dot her flesh. "Not gonna lie," she moans, "I feel pretty damn lucky right now."

"And I feel like we both won the good-guy chal-lenge," I say.

She smiles, soft and sex-drunk. "We both did. In multiple categories."

I'm buzzing from the high of knowing I brought her pleasure—hell, from the sensation of my own pleasure.

So that's great sex.

I finally found it.

Only, what made it so great is that I'm pretty sure I'm falling harder than I ever expected for London Hollis.

28

Early the next morning

From the Woman Power Trio, aka the text messages of London and her two besties, Olive and Emery

Olive: Soooooooooooooo . . .

Emery: *taps foot*

Olive: *waits, waits, waits*

Emery: *prepares to show up at Teddy's place and demand details*

London: Oh, hi! It's me! Waking up next to this guy I like.

Olive: I WANT ALL THE DETAILS.

Emery: AND NOW.

London: He has a tattoo.

Olive: Hot. Go on.

London: I spent the night. So did my dog. The sex was intense, the conversation incredible, and . . . I'm falling for him, and I'm pretty sure he's falling for me too.

Olive: So basically all that stuff about him not wanting more because of your brother and blah, blah, blah is out the window?

London: Ummmmm, maybe?

Emery: Whoa. This is huge.

London: I know, right? And I'm going to have to say something to Archer soon . . . but I want to figure out what this is first.

Olive: Smart. But can we rewind to the hot sex stories first and then do the wedding registry?

London: He's waking up. More later!

29

Waking up feels better than it has in a long time. It's for two reasons, I'd wager.

First—the great-sex effect.

I had it last night, and it was fucking awesome.

Plus, the aftereffects last till dawn.

Who knew?

That should be on the list of side effects of great sex —*you'll still feel fantastic in the morning.*

But there's another reason.

An even better reason.

My arms are wrapped around London as my eyes open. It's a helluva way to start a day—with London's rear nestled against my groin.

Why, yes, I'll avail myself of this side effect too, thank you very much.

London grinds her hips into me on a low moan, then reaches over to the nightstand and grabs a condom.

My hand on her hip slides gently toward her center, where she's warm, wet, and just as ready for this as I am.

Taking the condom, I sheath myself and slide into her from behind, pumping slowly to give her time to accommodate my length.

With one of my hands cupping her breast, we move together under the covers, feeling each other from this new angle. It's not long before we're coming together, and it's fantastic.

I always knew morning sex was going to be awesome. I'm glad to finally have the proof.

"And now, I'm hungry for food," London murmurs.

"Ravenous," I agree.

We get out of bed, brush our teeth—shout out to my dentist for the drawer full of unused toothbrushes—and leash up the dogs for a quick walk.

As I clip the leash on Bowie, my phone pings with an alert. Sliding my thumb across the screen, I grin as I read a response to Bloom's Yelp review.

A request for another wedding booking. "Yes!"

"Let me guess. You got a coupon for a free scoop at McConnell's today too?"

"That is indeed cause for celebration, but so's this," I say, showing her the review.

She beams, her whole face lighting up with pride. Damn, that looks good on her. And it feels good, too, to elicit that reaction. "Teddy, I am so excited for you," she says in a way that hooks into my heart.

"Thanks. Me too. I'm stoked. I've had two new booking requests this morning from her review. So things are looking up." I rap twice on the doorframe for luck.

"It's not luck. You're good at what you do."

"So are you," I say.

She blows on her fingernails as she wraps the dog's leash around her other wrist. "Look at us. Making things happen. My routine is almost ready to present to Archer and the partners, and to use in my portfolio, and you're on a fast track to becoming LA's premiere wedding and event DJ," she says.

When she puts it like that, everything feels possible.

Everything including being with her.

Perhaps that *maybe someday* isn't so far away.

We leave with the dogs. On the landing, the rattling of pans from inside Sherri's home reaches my ears, so I give the door a quick knock to see if Vin Scully needs a trip outside. Sherri hands her dog over in no time.

"Buenos días, oso," she says, greeting me, and then she catches sight of London as she's clipping Vin's collar. "Oh, is this the *guapa* you were telling me about?"

"Sí, Sherri. Por favor, no me avergüences. This is London," I say, and after a brief introduction and a suggestive smile from Sherri, my sleepover companion and I head down the hall.

"*Guapa*? Is that good or bad?" London asks.

"It means 'beautiful.' I told her that you are, because . . . *duh.* Then I asked her not to embarrass me." A slight flush heats my cheeks.

"Too late," London says with a smile.

Yeah, it's too late for a lot of things.

Like turning back.

That's both the good news and the bad news.

* * *

Thirty minutes later, we arrive at my favorite breakfast spot.

"House of Pies? I didn't know it was dessert for breakfast day, but sign me up."

"Far be it for me to tell you not to have pie for breakfast, but they do have other things on the menu. That's where they get their name." I point to a glorious glass case full of pies next to the register. It sparkles like a shrine to sugar.

We stand at the door, since Mr. Darcy is with us. A hostess swings by with an *aww, cutie* for the pooch, asking if we're three or two.

"Two, and one under the table."

"He's so handsome," she says to the dog.

"Thank you. He knows it too," London says.

"Good for him. Body confidence is so important in this city."

"Couldn't agree more," London says.

The hostess shows us to a table outside, where Mr. Darcy tucks himself under London's seat.

Soon, the waiter swings by, offering coffee. We both nod, and he fills our cups. After we order a pair of egg white omelets and he takes off for the kitchen, I offer a toast.

"To great sex."

"That's awfully presumptuous of you, Mr. Lockhart."

"Not complimenting myself. Complimenting you and the way you made me feel."

She grins. "The feelings are indeed mutual. So there."

"Good to know."

"So . . .?" She leaves the unasked question dangling.

I grab hold of the opportunity. "We should do that again. And I mean the sex, but also everything else. Like this. Hanging out together the next morning. Going for dog walks. Listening to music. Talking. All of it." I'm laying it all on the line, and nerves rise up in me.

But it's worth facing those nerves.

Because I want what's on the other side.

That's the thing about great sex—it's great because it's not just sex.

It's connection.

Intimacy.

Feelings.

I feel so much for this woman.

And I need to make room in my life for her. How to do that is another matter, but I'm determined to figure it out.

Especially since the universe is aligning and seems to be on my side.

If my event entertainment company can grow quickly, like it's trending now, maybe I don't need to worry about the risks of dating my boss's sister.

Maybe he won't be my boss for much longer.

He asked me to give him a heads-up about leaving. With gigs coming through, maybe that time is coming any day now. And sure, it's a risk—I'd be walking away from a regular paycheck for a few gigs. But I'd still have the radio show, and maybe this is the push I need. The push to take the leap, to hustle harder, to make this thing work if it's what I really want.

Then I won't have to face the music.

I can simply slide out in the nick of time, like

Indiana Jones snagging his hat before the boulder can crush it.

Or him.

Yup, I'll be Indy.

I draw a deep breath. "What if we see each other for the next few days, maybe even the next week, and that should be enough time for me to sort things out with my career?"

She frowns. "I think that sounds great, but I do want to tell my brother that I'm seeing you. I feel like I'm keeping something from him."

My gut twists, guilt winging through me. "Shit, London. I'm sorry. I didn't think about that. About you keeping stuff from him. I don't want to put you in that position."

"It's okay. I didn't think about it much myself until the last few days, when it felt like we might become something. But now it seems that way, and I don't want to keep a secret from my brother. A secret that affects him."

"Of course. I get it. I do."

"If he were in town, I'd honestly want to tell him today. But he has that camping thing."

Ding, ding, ding!

"That camping thing" might buy me some time. A few days to get my ducks in a row.

This is the kick in the pants I need. I can't ask London to keep her lips zipped. And I definitely don't want to break things off. But we have a couple days to sort this out while Archer is unplugged.

Maybe the answer is a simple one.

"This might be crazy, but if everything keeps going my way, I could give notice on Friday when Archer is back. Then I'd leave the club in a few weeks, and I wouldn't have to worry about mixing business and pleasure. Know what I mean?"

Her smile spreads nice and easy. "I do. But quitting is a big deal. Are you ready for that?"

I rap my knuckles against the table. "Business is taking off. Seems like my time to fly." The way I see it is I'll give notice, finish out the job, then find the right time to tell Archer I'm dating his sister. But it won't be a conflict of interest anymore.

She reaches for my hand and squeezes. "As long as you're doing it for you." I tense for a second, but she squeezes tighter. "Because you should do it for you. I know you like your job."

"My job is fun. But it's also not my endgame. So it's time to start my endgame sooner. And you're part of that reason."

"I can't argue with that. And of course I want to be with you. I'm so into you. I can't believe it's been less than two weeks, but I just am."

There she goes again.

Making me feel like I'm on top of the world.

"You're doing everything to me, London." I lean across the table to drop a kiss onto her lips. She kisses me back, soft and slow, and it goes to my head.

To my heart.

Makes me feel like all these plans are possible.

That luck is real.

When I break the kiss, she's still smiling. "Before I

met you, I wanted to just focus on my career," she says. "Find some great opportunities. But then you showed up at the dog park and . . . well, I like you a lot, Teddy. I want to see where this can go."

Ah, hell.

I might be swooning right now—melting here at the table.

I like this woman so much.

Although it's so much more than like.

"Good. Because I'm thinking we should now take on the dating challenge, the sixty-nine challenge, and the getting-to-know-you-even-more challenge," I say, and we both break out in stupid grins.

"I'm up for all of those."

Our eggs arrive, and as we eat, we geek out over the recent science podcast episode about why microwaves cook from the outside in, as London feeds bits of melon to Mr. Darcy.

It's a perfect morning to cap off a perfect few days.

And I feel like the luckiest guy in Los Angeles.

Nothing and no one can change my luck.

Of that I'm sure.

So sure that we don't even order dessert. If I play these cards right, I should be able to have my career and London too.

And that's a hell of a lot tastier than pie.

30

On Tuesday evening, London and Mr. Darcy make a welcome return to my place. The dogs enjoy a rawhide on Bowie's spot on the floor, which he's graciously sharing with the little dude, while London and I dine on grilled chicken salads that I ordered from a great café down the street.

What? Cooking is hard.

London edges me out, three games to two, in a *Jeopardy!* marathon, and we end the night with some marathon sex. We both win at that.

After I meet with my new clients on Wednesday to prep for their events, London and I spend the afternoon at her place fine-tuning the set list for her video shoot while I admire her moves, her curves, and her sexy-as-sin work ethic.

"I can't wait to show off this routine to Edge ownership," she says, breathing hard, but smiling harder. "And then to see the dancers put it in motion."

"The crowds are going to love it. The partners will

love it. And so will Archer," I say, but I nearly choke on the name.

I'll give him notice in two more days, and then I'll be on my way to everything I want—the career, the woman, and the life.

That evening, we play mini-golf then go to her place. The dogs are officially besties now, and there's nothing cuter than my fifty-pound bruiser cuddling with his teacup companion. I'm quite partial to snuggling up to Mr. Darcy's owner too, which we do that night.

Then we practice some new choreography. But these moves are just for the two of us.

On Thursday, I wake with a knot coiling in my chest, mixed emotions swirling through my head.

Sure, my side hustle is firing on all cylinders, and so is this *thing* with London. But that only amps up my need to move on from Edge, which has to wait till Archer returns from his oxymoronic corporate camping excursion. That should be a relief—having to wait just twenty-four more hours—but I feel like I'm living on borrowed time, waiting to be called into the principal's office.

But that's silly. I can't be called in, since he's out of town. I'll get the jump on him and talk to him the second he returns.

I try to narrow my thoughts on that plan.

I spend the morning hiking with Bowie, but the clear blue skies do nothing to get me out of this haze.

After, I work on my playlists for my upcoming events, send out another round of inquiries, email my new clients, then make my way to Edge.

Once there, I help with the prep work for London's performance. The playlist is cued up on the club speakers that are set to auto-fade while I stand in front of the stage, phone camera ready to film her work.

She moves through Nirvana, Taylor Swift, Imagine Dragons, Duran Duran, and Survivor with grace, power, and sex appeal.

I hope the camera captures her raw magnetism and electric sensuality as palpably as I can feel it live.

When she's done, I stop the recording and slide the phone into my pocket. Then I start a slow clap, long and proud.

London, only slightly out of breath, smiles when she says, "For real? You liked it?"

"Loved it. That was incredible. Seriously amazing."

She beams and then throws her arms around me.

I wince, wishing I could linger in a hug with London for hours, but we need to keep our distance at the club until we can sort everything out.

"Hey, watch the sweat, woman," I tease to create some distance between us.

"Right, right. I'm covered in it," she says with a laugh. Then she sighs, relieved. "That felt good. The performance."

"Because it was. You're better than us."

Stanley's voice booms across the club as he appears

in the main room, Carlos by his side. Stanley's not normally the loud one, so I tilt my head, curious.

"You saw that?" I ask.

"Saw it. Loved it."

"Did you really?" London chimes in, eager perhaps for feedback from another dancer.

"So much that I'll be coming here as a patron too," Stanley says with a big, genuine grin.

"Me too, and that's saying something," Carlos puts in. "Very sexy. If you're into ladies."

"Some men are," Stanley adds with a shrug, softer this time, his usual tone.

"Takes all kinds," Carlos says, then moves closer, bumping hips with London. "We'll have to work on a dance someday, girl. You've got the moves."

"Name the time and place, and I'm there," she says, and I'm grinning too as London basks in the moment and the praise from all quarters.

Then she goes right into work mode. "Okay, Teddy. Let's get that video edited and uploaded so I can start sharing it with some casting directors and choreographers, and Archer, of course."

"I'm on it, boss," I say, loving this take-charge side of London.

"And assuming Archer likes the concept—" she says.

"Which he totally will," Stanley cuts in.

"I hope so. Then we can start prepping the next steps on this thing," London continues. "Hire dancers, rehearse, promote."

"Can't wait to see it," Carlos says, and he and Stanley head to the dressing room.

London turns to me, her eyes full of gratitude. "I couldn't have done this without you. Thank you. For everything."

"The pleasure has been mine." We're alone in the club for the moment, the joint unusually quiet.

"Mine too," she says in a soft, barely audible whisper that makes me shiver.

My body sways a little closer to hers, but I determinedly resist the urge to kiss her. Her smile tells me resistance is hard for her too.

But we won't have to do it for much longer.

Tomorrow, I'll make the first move—set the wheels in motion so that in a few weeks' time, we can come clean.

It's risky, but I'm ready.

It's time for me to do my own thing.

And then to get the girl.

31

The woman I want crosses one ankle over the other, lounging seductively at an outdoor table as the sun streams across the sidewalk.

Then again, everything she does is seductive to me.

She could clean the kitchen counter and look hot.

As I near her, London pops her purple sunglasses up on her head and shoots me a smile.

I give her a curious look as I join her at House of Pies the next morning. I worked too late to see her last night.

"Purple shades? An homage to Prince?" I ask when I reach her table.

"Or maybe it's my favorite color when I'm in a particularly good mood," she says, rising from her chair.

That's my invitation to slide in for a kiss.

I cup her cheek, press a kiss to her soft lips, and imagine we'll do this every day.

We break the contact and sit. "So, purple is your favorite color. I can't believe I didn't know this," I say.

"We need to rectify this right now. I need all sorts of favorites from you."

"Ooh, a rectification. I'm down for that. Also, how dirty does that word sound? As dirty as, say, flange or masticate?"

"Or bilabial fricative."

She blinks, then narrows her eyes. "Wash your mouth out with soap."

"I know, right? Sounds filthy."

"Sounds intriguing. What the flange is a bilabial fricative?" she asks, but before I can answer, a waiter stops by.

We order eggs and coffee, and thank him.

Once he leaves, I answer London. "I wish it were a wild new position I could introduce you to. It's just a type of consonant sound. But it's one of those things I learned from having to, ya know, use my voice for a living."

"If you want some dirty-sounding jargon from my profession, I can offer coccyx balance."

I lean closer, lowering my voice. "I'd like to balance you on my cock."

She laughs. "I knew you wouldn't be able to resist that."

"You were right. But don't let me distract you from the rectification. Tell me stuff."

She taps her glasses. "These are my prescription shades, because purple is my favorite color. But sometimes red is too. You know my favorite food is sushi and that I pledge my allegiance to ice cream. I should probably add that my favorite movie of all time is *Ten Things*

I Hate About You because Heath Ledger can sing and act, and I love the nineties, which you know because of my *90210* shirt. And I bet it won't surprise you to know that my favorite book is *Pride and Prejudice*," she says, and I grin like a lovestruck fool because I knew some of that, but not all, and I fucking love learning things about this woman.

Love.

There's that word.

I think I'm more than falling for her.

I think I'm falling into something I didn't expect to happen.

"More, gimme more. I'm hungry for London intel," I say.

"If you insist, here's another tidbit. Did you know I'm excellent at ballroom dancing?"

I laugh. "No, but I'm not surprised."

"Tango is my favorite, and that's why I'm excited today and wearing my purple glasses."

"For your good mood?"

"Yes, because I got a fantastic email this morning. It's about a job."

"The one with André Davies? The producer?"

She shakes her head. "No, it's from Shay Sloan. The woman I worked with in Vegas."

A sliver of worry spreads under my skin. "Are you going back to Vegas?"

She laughs, shaking her head. "No. But she recommended me for a job in San Francisco, and she said the director of that show is interested in talking to me today about a ballroom dancing sequence in a musical he's producing. And if all goes well, he'll fly me out ASAP for a trial and to see if I like the city."

This is awesome.

And a little alarming.

"To see if you like San Francisco?" I ask, since that's a twist I didn't see coming. "Did you know that was going to happen?"

"I had no idea. I just got an email. He wants to talk on the phone later today, so we set up a call."

I swallow, trying to figure out what to say next, how to be the supportive . . . boyfriend?

Since I think that's what I'm supposed to be.

"That's really fantastic," I say, meaning it, but also trying to figure out what the hell this San Francisco job means for us.

She reaches for my hand, threading her fingers through mine. "But don't worry. I still want to see you. Whatever happens with the job."

Fuck, do I even deserve her?

I want it to be tomorrow so I can begin to sort this out.

I need to get my shit together and stop playing What's Your Favorite Color games, even though I love knowing all her favorite things.

Because I love . . .

A brash voice cuts across the morning air. "Goooooood morning, Insomnia!"

I jerk my gaze from London as Carlos calls out in a distinct Robin Williams impersonation. How does he have this much energy after a full night of working the pole?

The smoothie in his hand is my only guess. He's a few feet away, walking toward us with Stanley, both of them in muscle tanks and gym shorts.

"Hey," I say, my back straightening as a bolt of tension shoots through me. London and I are only having breakfast, but we *were* kissing, and she *was* holding my hand, and fuck me.

I need to figure my shit out fast because I don't want to run into anyone from work here. Don't want to see anyone before I tell Archer I'm going to leave and then date his sister.

Maybe they won't notice who I'm with. Or, hey, maybe they'll walk right on past us without glancing her way or saying another word.

No such luck. The two big men stop at our table.

"Lookie look. It's my new dance partner. When are we going to work on our routine?" Carlos asks, bending to drop a kiss onto London's cheek. Never let it be said that Carlos takes a long time to make friends.

"It better be soon. I saw you dance a few weeks ago, and you have got some serious hip action," she says.

Carlos's brown eyes twinkle, then he nudges Stanley. "See? Told you I was a better dancer than you."

Stanley narrows his eyes. "I don't think that's what she said."

"That's what I heard." Carlos's eyes flick to me and back to London, like he's processing the scene fully. And process it he does.

"Ohhhhhh. You two are together. Holy shit. I didn't know you were dating the boss's sister," he says, smacking my shoulder.

Fuck. My. Life.

London shoots me a look that says *Fix this*.

But before I can say a word, Stanley cuts in. "Oh, the scandal of it all," he says, as though the two of them are on a daytime soap.

Carlos sweeps his hand in front of him like he's framing a marquee. "Tune in at three for the latest drama on *As the Edge Turns*."

I groan, my chest tightening, my gut coiling. "All right, guys, it's just breakfast," I say, hoping to end their fun.

But they won't be denied.

"And people who have breakfast together usually had dinner together the night before," Carlos says to Stanley.

"And probably dessert too," Stanley fires back.

"We're just talking about work stuff," I say, nearly choking on the lameness of my reply.

Carlos claps my shoulder. "We're just messing with you, buddy. You two enjoy your *work breakfast*. See you at the club tonight."

"And no worries, Teddy. Your secret's safe with us," Stanley says like he's in a cheesy horror film, and the two head off.

My skin prickles with nerves.

No, worse—with guilt.

As they walk away, I turn to face London. Her brown eyes display her worry too.

I groan, the loudest groan in the city, then drop my face to the table. "I'm such an ass."

Running into my coworkers for breakfast and lying

to them? How the hell did I get to this point?

Oh, right. By trying to hedge my bets.

A soft hand strokes my hair. "You're not an ass. But maybe . . ."

I lift my face. "Maybe I am?"

She shakes her head. "No. But maybe if you feel that way, we should . . ."

She doesn't have to finish the thought—I do. I hate what I'm about to say, but I have to say it. "Cool things off?" It comes out strangled. Hell, the words are choking me.

She nods, her gaze full of sympathy. "I don't want to, but I get why you feel crummy. You've been honest with me about where you're coming from. I know that mixing work and relationships is tough for you."

"So we should cool it?" I ask, needing the confirmation, needing to say it aloud, so it registers fully.

"Maybe? Probably," she says heavily.

My heart sinks like an anchor in my chest. Because she's right. I've been honest with her, but I haven't been honest with Archer. And that's on me. I knew I was playing with fire. I was living on borrowed time, a mouse playing while the cat was away. But that's not how you tell someone something hard.

There's a right way to do things.

To say the hard stuff.

Seeing the guys is the splash of cold water I needed. I can't keep having my cake and eating it too simply because of a fucking camping trip.

Archer unplugged is a reprieve, but it's not permission.

I thought I had set my defenses up to protect against this possibility. All I had to do was meet a woman from outside my place of business. Keep work and my private life separate. In Los Angeles, of all places, that shouldn't have been difficult. Then I met London. And now she's the only woman I want.

Trouble is, I haven't earned her yet.

If I'm going to take the good-guy challenge in bed, I need to behave like one outside of the bedroom too. That means doing the right thing, even when it's difficult.

I swallow roughly, then nod, owning this next step no matter how much it sucks. "I should sort things out," I say, doing my best to play it cool, like this is easy. Because I don't want to make anything harder for her.

Her face relaxes, her expression softening, like she's relieved. "That moment just now was a little too close for comfort. Maybe we both need to breathe."

"Absolutely. You've got this new opportunity in San Francisco. You should figure out what that means too."

"More than that, Teddy," London says softly, like she's forcing the words out. "I see how conflicted you are right now, and I don't want to be the one to stand in your way."

Her last line hits me square in the chest. But as much as I want to fight for us, she's right. "And I don't want to stand in your way either."

She glances inside toward the restaurant, then smacks her forehead. "I just remembered. I got the time wrong on that call. It's in a half hour. I better go and take it at home."

I blink, surprised. London usually remembers details like that. "Of course. Good luck."

"And to you too," she says, then grabs her purse, palms her keys, and stands.

What the hell do I do now? Hug her? Kiss her goodbye? Shake hands? "I'll talk to you soon?"

It comes out as a question, one neither of us can answer.

She shoots me a sad smile, then nods, spins on her heel, and walks away.

I groan in frustration, dragging a hand through my hair. I *don't know* when I will talk to her, because I'm pretty sure we just broke up.

And surer still that we needed to.

My stomach churns, and my head pounds.

I sink low in my chair, rubbing my hand across the back of my neck, wishing I could go back in time. Redo things. Change things. I don't even know.

Do *something* differently.

All along, I've been playing with fire, chasing a work high, a sex high, and then a falling-in-love high too.

But with all highs, there's a low. The higher you soar, the farther you fall.

And this is a bumpy ride back down.

A minute later, the waiter brings two plates of eggs, but I don't even have the stomach for one.

Especially when my phone buzzes and I check my email.

It's from the bride who just hired me.

Turns out she's postponing her wedding indefinitely.

Looks like in the span of ten minutes, I've lost a gig, the woman, and maybe even the job I already have.

In one damn morning, all my luck has drained away.

32

I do my best to focus on work after the world's worst morning. I'm tweaking some new online ads for my website when the phone rings later that day. Mom's picture lights up the display, and I answer immediately, grateful for a friendly voice.

Someone who's on my side.

"Hey, Mom," I say, setting my laptop on the coffee table.

"Have I ever told you what a charming and wonderful son your father and I think you are?"

"Mmm, flattery. Something must be broken." I know this routine, have played it for years. Today, it's weirdly comforting.

"The bathroom sink is completely clogged. I tried unscrewing a pipe—"

"Mom, what have I told you? Do not attempt handiwork."

"Yes, it did seem to cause more problems. But you're so clever and—"

"I'm on my way."

* * *

Ninety minutes later, I toss my wrench back in the tool-box, the job done. At least I did something right today.

"Good as new, Mom," I say, walking into the kitchen. "And I organized the towels under the bathroom sink."

She arches a brow. "You don't organize. Something must be off."

Everything is off.

"Least I could do," I say, grabbing my keys off the entryway table.

"Want to stay for some lemonade? Shame to come all this way just to turn around and drive home."

Pretty sure I don't deserve lemonade, but I can't resist. She makes it from scratch with vanilla and honey. "Sure."

"If all I get is a *sure* to the one thing that you'd beg, borrow, and steal anything to have, I'm guessing you're having a bad day. What's wrong, sweetie?"

I heave a sigh. The saddest one in the country. "Might be easier to tell you what's right," I say, taking a seat on a barstool by the island.

Mom pours me a glass of lemonade as I serve up the sad, sorry state of my heart. "London and I broke up today."

Her brow knits. "I didn't know you were dating anyone. You said the other day you weren't."

My shoulders sag. I suck, and lemonade won't fix it. I lied to my parents. "Yeah, sorry, Mom. I didn't want to say anything, because she's kind of off-limits," I say, then give her the details. The PG version. "So what started as a simple date turned into a complicated thing, because her brother is my boss and the lines were getting blurry."

"That sounds familiar," she says gently, leaning on the island opposite me.

"It feels familiar. But also not. The circumstances are definitely reminiscent of Tracy, but my feelings for London are decidedly different." I take a drink of the lemonade. "This is delicious," I say, enjoying the simplicity of the drink. The constancy. Then I soldier on, too much to get off my chest now that the flood-gates have opened.

"I'd convinced myself that we could make it work because my event company was picking up steam since the last time we talked. Then one of my bookings canceled this morning, I don't know where I stand with the job I already have, and now I've lost the woman too."

Mom cuts right to the chase. "Do you love her?"

The answer flutters to life in my gut the second she asks. I try to think it through, to apply logic, but my body knows instantly—it longs for London. I met her two weeks ago, and she's fantastic, open, fun, passion-ate, supportive, and the coolest person ever. But there's even more than that.

We spark.

On pretty much everything.

From dogs, to tacos, to Instant Pots.

From kissing, to connecting, to spending time together.

Every moment with her is electric, in bed and out of bed.

And that's awesome and terrible at the same damn time.

Because I *really* need to figure things out.

And fast.

I give my mom a helpless smile. "I think I've fallen in love with her."

Mom smiles, but it doesn't last long. "Sounds like you still have a lot to work out. Finding a career of value and substance is important. The same can be said of finding a partner. As long as you're honest with yourself first, you'll figure out what to do next."

I hope I figure it out soon, since I'm going into work in a few more hours.

* * *

My mom's advice clangs around in my head on the drive home. I want to do the right thing, one step at a time, but my life is a Jenga tower right now, teetering on a bunch of center blocks.

As I walk into my place, my normally boisterous door greeter doesn't even look up. He keeps gnawing on his hedgie in his spot.

"Hey, buddy. Did you miss me?"

He jerks his head away and kills the toy even more dead.

I flop down on the couch. "Tell me what to do next."

Bowie is usually a good listener, but he shakes the hedgie another time, focused only on the toy.

Great. My dog won't even amateur psychoanalyze me now.

I take a shower to clear my head, but the heat and the steam don't bring answers about what to do next.

I text Sam to see if I can stop by his place before work. He says yes.

Ten minutes later, Sam lets me into his living room, where a yoga mat and blocks dominate the space.

"Didn't mean to interrupt your practice."

"All good, brother. Your text came in the middle of my vinyasa. Normally I'm too centered to deal with my phone, but something told me you needed me. Almost like your reaching out was a part of the flow, know what I mean?"

My brow knits in confusion. Hell, my whole body is a pretzel, and not the yoga kind. "I don't know what anything means right now, man."

"Whoa, slow down, bro. What's going on? Sit."

I take a seat on his couch as he returns to the floor, holding court, listening attentively in half lotus. I catch him up on everything: London, running into the guys this morning, losing an All Night Entertainment gig. "And now I'm not even sure where I stand with Archer and the club—the one thing that's been a constant for me this past year, and I've probably fucked that up too. All because, out of the four million people in LA, I happened to fall in love with the one woman related to my boss."

"Ten million, actually."

"What?" I ask, confused.

"Four million people in the city, but ten million in LA county. You found the one in a sea of ten million."

"Oh. Sounds romantic and star-crossed when you say it like that."

Sam takes a deep, even breath and slowly lets it out. "It kinda is, Teddy. Think about all the possible moments in your life that can set off sparks. All the interactions that could ignite something fierce. And after Tracy, you were actively trying *not* to let that fire happen at work again, but it did. What you and London have is undeniable, man. Unavoidable. You just told me you loved her. Didn't even flinch."

"Because I do," I say, the gravity of my words more intense than before.

I love London.

I want to go to weddings with her, take her out for sushi, bring the dogs to the park, eat ice cream, talk about toasters.

Everything is better with London.

Trouble is, London's gone. She needs space.

And truthfully, I need it too.

But I don't know what to do now, so I hold my arms out wide. "What do I say to Archer tonight? Do I quit? Do I tell him I'm in love with his sister? I've been down this road before, and it didn't end well."

Sam adjusts his other leg on top of his half lotus. "London's not Tracy, and Archer isn't Tracy's dad. None of this has ever happened before. Every moment is new. What does your gut tell you? What does your heart say? Ask those questions and listen to the answers. Then decide what you're going to do with *this* moment."

I mull over his advice, but not for long.

Because ideas begin to spark.

Plans take shape.

Real ones. True ones.

"I need to be honest." I recall Mom's advice about priorities, and as Sam's wisdom also takes hold, so does my certainty. "I need to come clean." The thoughts pour out as fast as they form. "Not just about the job. I need to be fully honest with my boss. I owe it to him. I owe it to London. Hell, I owe it to myself. Because that's the man I want to be. A good guy." I smile, remembering London's initial challenge to me.

"That's the Teddy I've always known, but life is a series of tests we must continually pass."

Energy fills me, flooding my cells. My mind races to tonight.

I stand. Pace. Blueprint the evening ahead.

"I need to quit Edge, but not for the reasons I thought. I thought I could quit, then mention I was seeing London down the road, and it wouldn't be a big deal. But she's not a 'down the road' person. She's right fucking now." I pace in the other direction, ticking off points as I talk. "I need to quit because having my own company is my dream. I can't be the man I need to be for London if I'm not the man I want to be for myself. And that starts by telling my boss the truth and taking a chance on myself."

It's time to give everything I have to a company that hasn't even taken flight yet. But the risk will be worth it. I believe that.

I blow out a heavy sigh. "This won't be easy."

Sam nods sagely. "It's like Bodhi tells Johnny in *Point Break*: 'If you want the ultimate, you've got to be willing to pay the ultimate price.'"

I stare at him, noodling on that. He's right. Like Bodhi was right. "I needed that. Thanks, man."

I smile and give Sam a big hug before I leave, knowing what I need to do next.

It's time to take control of my life. Even if it means losing a lot along the way.

33

On the one hand, this is a death march.

On the other, I'm walking into my future.

That's what I tell myself as I administer an epic pep talk on the drive to work. Sam, riding with me in the car, backs me up.

"You've got this," he says as I turn onto the block that houses Edge. "You've so got this, bro."

"Thanks, man. I appreciate all the help today. I couldn't have figured this out without you."

Sam shakes his head, having none of it. "Nope. It's all you."

At Edge, I park my car, cut the engine, and scan the lot.

My stomach leaps into my lungs when I spot Archer's red Lexus here. That's a good sign, but it's also an omen that shit is about to get real.

It's hard to leave a job you like, to say goodbye to a boss who's been good to you. "I can do this," I say as I head toward the club, Sam by my side.

"You can do it, just like I can do a hot AF dance to 'You Shook Me All Night Long.'"

"True. You can definitely do that."

"So if you need extra guts before you go into his office, just think about me shaking my hips to that rock anthem."

"I probably won't do that, but I do appreciate the offer," I say dryly.

"Just trying to help a brother out."

I open the door to the club, both nervous and resolute. I'm ready for my future.

For everything.

As Sam makes his way to the dressing rooms, I head around the corner to the manager's office.

Archer's voice drifts through the doorway, sounding like he's finishing a phone call. My shoulders tense as he says, "Sounds great. Talk to you again soon."

The tension spreads as reality kicks all the way in once I reach his office. I'm doing this. True, I'm stepping into my future, but it's without a safety net.

I knock on the open door as Archer ends the call then flashes me a professional grin. "Hey, Teddy. How's everything going?"

"Good," I say, my pitch a little high. I draw a breath, trying to keep my voice even, but I don't budge from the doorway. "Do you have a minute?"

His brow knits. "Sure. I was hoping to chat with you too."

He wants to talk to me too? About what? My tongue feels heavy, my throat dry.

Archer waves me in. "Come in. You look like this is a take-a-seat conversation."

I nod, relieved that he senses my awkwardness. "It is, sir."

He blows out a long stream of air. "You're breaking out the *sir*. Sounds more like it's a shut-the-door conversation."

"Yes, it is," I say, turning around, doing just that, then grabbing a seat in the chair across from his desk. He waits, his expression patient.

Time for me to man up.

I draw a breath, letting it fuel me. "You said the other week that if I wanted to pursue other opportunities, you would just be grateful for a heads-up."

He winces. His expression falters. "I did." He leans back in his chair. "I had a feeling this was coming."

I run my palms along my jeans. "I'd like to give you my two weeks' notice. I didn't think it would come so soon, but the thing is, I really want to run my own company," I say, getting those words out finally, and once I do, I feel lighter, buoyant. "I want to do weddings. I want to do bar mitzvahs. I want to do celebrations. I want to be part of these great family rituals. Parties, birthdays, anniversaries—that's what I really like doing."

He nods a few times. "I can see that in you. That seems like your jam."

"It is. The wedding I did last weekend reminded me of that. Honestly, even helping choreograph London's routine reminded me how much I like putting music together for all sorts of opportunities. And I think I should devote all of my attention to that kind of work," I say, taking a staggered breath after getting all those words out. All those true words that I should've said a few days ago. But it took me that time to figure out what I needed for my own happiness.

Archer picks up a pen, spinning it between his thumb and forefinger. "I'll miss having you around here, but I appreciate you coming to me. I had a feeling that was what you wanted to talk about as soon as you showed up in my doorway."

I swallow, digging down deep to say the next thing. "But there's something else I need to chat with you about too."

He makes a rolling gesture with his hand that translates to *go ahead*. "You've got the floor."

I rip off the Band-Aid. "I've been seeing London."

His eyes widen to the size of pizza pies. But he says nothing.

That's okay. I have more to say. More that I *should* say. "I didn't expect anything to happen. But I met her here at the club two weeks ago, and then I ran into her at the dog park before I knew she was related to you. I took her out to dinner, and I know I'm not supposed to be involved with people who work at the club, and more than that, she's your sister. I'm pretty sure it's a violation of the bro code to date your boss's sister," I say in a six-car verbal pileup.

Archer blinks. "Bro code. That's funny."

Is it funny? No idea. I still can't read him. I'm still not sure what he's thinking.

"But I did it anyway because she's fantastic, she's

brilliant, and I'm pretty much crazy about her," I say, starting with the *crazy about her* sentiment because I don't want to shock the guy further with the L word. "And I want to keep seeing her."

He's quiet. Too quiet. He doesn't say anything for several long seconds that threaten to spill into a minute.

An interminable minute.

Say something. Please say something.

He takes a deep breath, then speaks at last. "Is that why you're quitting?" he asks, like he's trying to make sense of all these events.

Understandable.

"No, and yes. I do think this is the next step of my career. And I also care deeply for her."

He runs a hand across his chin. "Well, that does make things a little more complicated with what I was going to talk to you about."

"What were you going to talk to me about?"

He parts his lips to speak, when his phone rings. He glances at the caller ID. "This is the call I was waiting for. I need to take it. I'll catch up with you at the end of the night though."

I leave with absolutely no clue what happens next.

34

That evening

From the Woman Power Trio, aka the text messages of London and her two besties, Olive and Emery

London: Makeup is magic.

Olive: Girl, I tell that to my mascara every day.

Emery: I'm convinced lipstick has special powers. The power to make me actually look decent every single day. But does this mean you're feeling better after this morning? You were pretty damn sad. Understandably.

Olive: Yeah, and if you're not feeling better, I am ready with my jujitsu skills to take the bastard down.

London: Appreciate the martial arts support, but no need for that. Also, "better" is relative. But I've applied mascara, so I look half human.

Olive: Then why are you not at my bar right now? Come hang out with me while I sling drinks, and you'll be fully human again.

Emery: I'm thinking a gal is more like one-quarter human after an Olive drink, and three-quarters happy alien moonwalking.

Olive: That is true. I am a badass bartender who delivers happy-alien-moonwalking libations. And badass bartenders also give excellent advice to their sad friends to help them be *unsad*. So get your cute butts here, ladies.

Emery: We need girl time. We need to help our London recalibrate.

Olive: Recalibration begins in thirty minutes!

London: On my way. Let me just grab some tissues and hug Mr. Darcy one more time.

Emery: Awww.

London: But I'll be fine. Plus, I need to figure out what to do about the San Francisco job, so we can chat about that.

Olive: You do. Because you kick ass at what you do. See you in thirty.

London: Smack me if I'm too sad, please?

Emery: There will be no smacking. You will get bestie hugs instead.

London: Shut up. I love you.

Olive: I love you so much that I'm turning your phone off when you arrive.

London: Deal.

35

The music thumps. Sam dances to "You Shook Me All Night Long" for Lydia's bachelorette party.

Carlos, Stanley, and the other guys join him onstage.

The women in the audience cheer and clap, tossing bills and toasting their friends.

The crowd is raucous, as they should be.

Tonight is everything Edge has always been.

In some ways, I'll miss it.

In most ways, I won't.

What I'll truly miss is the camaraderie with the guys. The ribbing, the jokes, the bro talk. The way the dancers rely on each other, and on me. How we look out for each other in this odd job we've found ourselves in. Usually, strip clubs are the butt of jokes, and dancers are seen as sex workers.

These guys though? They're just guys making a living.

Sam likes to move.

Stanley likes the extra money.

Carlos loves to dance.

No doubt I'll hang with them occasionally once I'm gone. For sure, Sam will always be in my life.

I check the time on my phone, willing the minutes to pass, wanting to know what Archer has to say next so I can wrap things up with him.

But at the same time, what can he say that'll change things? I already pulled the rip cord.

And survived.

I made my choice.

The other choice I want to make is *her*.

London.

I'm dying to see her again, touch her, kiss her.

Talk to her.

Figure out if we can take this thing off ice.

Heat it all the way up again.

Do I need to wait for Archer's nod of approval?

As soon as that thought lands, I dismiss it. This is my choice. Her choice. *Our* choice.

And I only want to choose her.

She's been on my mind all day long, and as the guys launch into a new routine Carlos choreographed to Sam Smith and Demi Lovato's "I'm Ready," I weigh my options.

Call London tomorrow? Text her? See her? Go to her place with a salted caramel ice cream cone and say, *Be mine*?

I lean back in my chair, contemplating, as the song echoes through the club.

As it does, I listen.

And I know.

The title can only be a message.

A command.

One I need to follow right this damn second.

I am ready.

Fuck waiting.

When you know you want to be with someone, when you know she's the one, you don't wait.

You *do*.

As the chorus blasts through the club, I open the message app on my phone and tap out a text to her.

Teddy: I can't stop thinking about you. I don't want to take a break from you any longer. I want to see you again. I want to talk to you. Tell you everything I figured out. Because I'm crazy for you, London. Text may not be the best way to tell you everything, but let me know if you're around.

I read it one more time, my finger hovering over the send button.

I am ready, no doubt.

But I've been learning that being ready means doing things right.

I'm not an expert on love, or women, or even great sex. But I've discovered this much from being with London and working out what I want.

A text isn't enough.

When you want to tell a woman you're in love with her, you need to show up in person.

Bring her a gift.

Do things the right way.

I hit delete.

* * *

The moment the last song of the night fades out, I grab my gear, tap the doorframe twice, then stop by Archer's office to finish our conversation.

But his door is shut.

I shrug. So it goes. He's not the priority any longer. London is. I'll catch up with him another day.

Sam waits by the front of the club, and I tell him I need to swing by Target before I head home.

"Sweet. I've been jonesing for some Cinnamon Life cereal, and Target has those big-ass boxes."

"Are you so hungry you're going to eat a whole box tonight?"

He frowns. "You're right. Six-packs don't grow on trees. I'll get some yogurt instead. Thanks for looking out for my abiliciousness."

"Yes, that's exactly what I was doing."

A little later, Sam is digging into his yogurt, I have a bag of home-baked dog treats in the center console, and we're cruising along the streets of Los Angeles after midnight on the way to London's house.

Sam hums thoughtfully. "Correct me if I'm wrong, but isn't it almost two in the morning?"

The green display on the car's dashboard confirms he can tell time. "It is."

"Does she want you to show up at two in the morning?"

I smile as I turn onto her street. "That's where this gift comes in."

"Oh. She's one of those women who likes you to leave gifts at two in the morning? I've heard of the existence of such ladies, but I haven't met any."

I roll my eyes. "I'm going to leave a gift on her doorstep. It feels like something a Jane Austen hero would do."

"Leave dog biscuits?"

"Yes. Captain Wentworth would, and he's the bomb," I say as I pull over, parking at the curb.

He seems to consider this, then nods. "Sure. I'm down with that. You're a regular Mr. Knightley."

I jerk my head back. "From *Emma*? Who *are* you?"

He scoffs. "Dude. How far do you think abs like these can take me? Only so far. Gotta back up the sixer with what's up here." He taps his temple. "I worship at the altar of Jane Austen. And for the record, Mr. Knightley wins. He was no bullshit with Emma. You should go the Knightley route." Sam adopts an aristocratic Victorian tone. "'I cannot make speeches, Emma . . . If I loved you less, I might be able to talk about it more. But you know what I am. You hear nothing but truth from me . . . Yes, you see, you understand my feelings.'"

"Is that what I should say to London?" I ask.

"No way." He smacks my sternum. "Don't recycle another dude's words. Speak from your heart."

That should be easy enough.

My heart is full for London.

I grab a pen from the glove box, scrawl out a sentence on the front of the bag, then bound up the lawn, around Nate and Eli's house, and over to London's studio.

I stop short when I see all the lights are off.

There is no barking pumpkin.

No London either. Where could she be? What if she left for San Francisco?

I shake my head. The interview was earlier today—no way would she have moved cities yet.

But that fear only reaffirms that I'm doing the right thing.

My heart hammers with worry as I set the bag down.

When she returns, she'll see my note.

Happiness in life is entirely a matter of dog biscuits. And finding the person you've fallen in love with.

36

The next morning, I'm up at dawn.

Sleep is for another day. Today is for action. Today is for finding the woman I love and telling her that even one more day apart from her is too much.

I do send her a text though.

Because, you know, details matter.

Teddy: Hey! Are you still here? Are you heading up to San Francisco for the job? I can't stop thinking about you, and I would love to see you. Ya know, today. 😃

She doesn't respond.

But it's early. And if this past week is anything to go by, she doesn't usually wake up till eight thirty. It's only seven.

But I am amped up. I throw the covers off, swing my

legs out of bed, head to the bathroom, brush my teeth, take a shower, and get ready for the day.

I leash up Bowie because he's part of the plan. Because dogs should always be part of the plan.

A little after eight, we leave my place, he jumps into the back seat of my car, and we make our way to the dog park.

The first time I saw London here, she told me she goes to this park every Saturday morning. So I'll wait for her. I have a tennis ball, a rawhide, and a hedgie, all with Mr. Darcy's name on them.

I scan the park. No sign of her, but it's still early.

I toss a ball to Bowie, over and over and over again.

For fifteen minutes, for twenty, for thirty.

Finally, my phone dings in my pocket, and my heart fucking soars above the stratosphere because it's a text from her.

London: I'm here in LA. I slept at Emery's last night with Mr. Darcy, and we're on our way to the dog park. Confession: I was so excited to get your text this morning. How are you?

How am I? I'm amazing. Because everything makes sense. Everything feels possible.

And then, everything is incredible when a few minutes later, a gorgeous, fantastic, bighearted brunette opens the gate into the dog park, red glasses on, a

Beverly Hills, 90210 shirt hugging her frame, and a blonde spitfire of a Chihuahua mix at her feet. London unclips his leash, and the teacup takes off, straight for Bowie.

I take off straight for her.

I'm grinning. My heart is flying.

I hope.

I hope so damn hard.

Five seconds, four seconds, three seconds, two, and then I'm right in front of her.

"I didn't expect to see you here," she says, but she can't seem to hide the happiness in her voice and the smile on her face.

Her eyes are curious though. She's waiting for me to take the next step.

That's on me. I'm the one who broke things off. I'm the one who has to let her know how I feel. "I left a gift for you at your house last night," I say. "But I'm guessing you didn't get it?"

"I didn't, but about ten minutes ago, Nate called and told me about it. I happen to love dog presents."

"It's for both of you," I say, and I want to tell her everything, but I need to start with an apology. I set a hand on her shoulder as the dogs play. It feels good to touch her again. "I'm sorry about yesterday morning at breakfast."

"Why are you sorry?"

"Because I said all the wrong things at all the wrong times."

She arches her brow as Mr. Darcy careens across the

park, Bowie racing behind him. The little dog arrives at our feet first. London reaches down, takes the tennis ball he brings her, and chucks it across the park. He takes off after it, and Bowie lumbers after him.

"What was wrong with the way you said things?"

I squeeze her shoulder then lift my hand and run my thumb along her jaw. She moves with me, a soft breath ghosting across her lips.

I inch closer. I'm not sure if I deserve her. I'm not sure if I've earned her. But I want to try. The only way to know is to put my heart on the line and tell her the truth.

"I like to think I'm a good guy. I want to believe I do the right things. But nobody can do that all the time, and I've had my share of fuckups over the last two weeks. There are things I should have done differently," I admit. I have my flaws, but I hope she wants me in spite of them. "But I *want* to do things differently from now on. The only thing I don't want to change is this—I don't want to lose you, London. You're more important to me than the job, than the club, than what happens next in my career."

Her eyes sparkle with happiness, a wild sort of joy filling them. "I don't want to lose you either," she says, and those words make everything better, knowing that we're in this together.

I sigh happily and sway closer to her, cupping her cheek. "I am so in love with you. And I don't want to lose you. Whatever happens next in my life, I want it to happen with you. And I hope you feel the same."

She grabs my face, draws me to her, and presses her lips to mine, giving me the softest, most wonderful kiss any man has ever received.

Then she pulls back. "I am so in love with you. And I want to figure everything out with you too."

Best day in the history of ever.

"You mean it? Even if you go to San Francisco for the job?"

Her smile is wide and bright. "Actually, I *am* heading to San Francisco for the job. I saw my friends last night, and I decided to go," she says.

A part of me doesn't want her to go, but a bigger part is thrilled for her. For this opportunity. For what it means for her career. "All right. What's the plan? I'll be there every weekend if you want me to. I'll fly you back down here."

She laughs, shaking her head. "You don't have to. I only took the job because it's for a month. It's a limited run. It's a great opportunity, and I'm super excited to do it. I took it knowing I'd be back here soon. My family is here, my friends are here, and you're here. And I believed that I'd be back together with you. If the job was longer than that, I would have said no."

I melt a little more for her, fall a little deeper, love a little harder. "You mean that?"

"Of course I mean it. I wouldn't take a job and move away even when we were on hold. I saw my friends last night, and I was bummed about us, but also hopeful. I know what we have is special, and I was going to come see you today and tell you that I'm crazy about you too."

My grin is bigger than this city. "More than crazy," I say, feeling like I'm walking on air.

"So much more than crazy," she says as Mr. Darcy scurries over along with David Bowie. They run circles around us, Bowie dropping the tennis ball this time, begging for someone to throw it.

I heed the dog call. I reach down, pick it up, and throw it across the park, then I gather London into my arms and kiss her once more.

Everything about this moment feels right. This is where I first talked to her in depth. This is where I first knew she was the woman I wanted to see.

Here we are again, giving this thing between us a real chance.

When I break the kiss, I run a hand through her hair. "Remember when you saw my tattoo?"

"I sure do."

I pull the sleeve up on my arm. "I've always been so fixated on the points, but I've never thought about that empty space created in the middle," I say, pointing to the spot. "Now I realize that spot's been waiting for you. Right there, in the center of me."

She grabs the neck of my shirt and pulls me closer. "That's exactly where I want to be," she says, and she smashes her lips to mine.

We pick up on that a little later, when we head to my place, toss some hedgies to the pups, then strip to nothing in seconds.

We move together, kissing, touching, loving.

A day with London that I never want to end.

But it does end because I need to work that night. I

have to finish out my commitment to Archer. He's not there, but that's okay. I do the job, and when I'm done I text London, and she meets me with her dog at my place.

Now this is a perfect end to a perfect day.

37

The dogs snore softly at the foot of the bed the next morning. London's eyes are still peacefully closed, her thigh draped over my leg. I could get used to this.

But my bliss is short-lived when I grab my phone, spotting a message from Archer asking if I can meet him for coffee this morning to finish our discussion. I check the clock then fire off a reply confirming the time and place.

I take a quick shower and throw on some clothes as London stirs in bed.

"Where are you going?" Her voice is all sleepy-sexy.

"I have a meeting with your brother. Shouldn't be long. Stay. Relax. I will return with coffee and bagels."

She smiles softly. "I'm so glad you didn't say muffins."

"Muffins are gigantic calorie bombs that can't commit to being cupcakes," I say. "If I want a cupcake, I'll get a cupcake."

"Exactly. Not a pale substitute. You get me," she says, watching me slip on my shoes.

"I do. I definitely do." I give her a kiss, then leave.

I open the door to the coffee shop, scanning the room for Archer. He's camped out in the corner, typing away on his laptop. Two steaming mugs sit on opposite ends of the small table.

"House roast, black. Right?" he asks as he gestures me into the other chair.

"That's exactly right. Thanks." I'm impressed he knows my order and consider it a good sign that he bought my drink. I slide into the chair, still confident that leaving Edge is the right decision, but curious as to what's on Archer's mind.

He closes his laptop, and his attention shoots squarely to me. "We didn't get a chance to finish our chat Friday night, but I'm glad I've had the time to think through things a bit more."

"I'm just glad you still want to speak to me," I say, half joking, sitting up a little straighter.

He smiles, but his focus remains locked in. "I know you're starting to branch out and do your own thing, and I respect that, but ownership had some exciting new developments to share during our camping retreat, and I'd like you to hear me out."

"I'm listening," I say.

"We're opening two new spaces in the city, with additional plans to expand up the coast. These won't be nightclubs—they're going to be event spaces. Weddings, corporate events, birthdays, and such."

Archer pauses to drum his fingers on the table. "What would you say to a contract position helping our company oversee bookings, communicating with clients, and organizing and staffing events? I speak for the owners when I say we'd be thrilled to have an exciting new start-up company under contract to help us manage these additional venues. In short, I want to know what I can do to make Edge Events a client of your new company."

I part my lips to speak, but I'm not entirely sure what to say. I'm floored. I take a drink of my coffee, digesting this unexpected offer. It's awesome, the chance to grow my business. Plus, the gig sounds like a ton of fun. But the best part is that Archer knows how I feel about London, and he still came to me with a work opportunity.

I look at my soon-to-be former boss, and my career worldview all clicks into place, and I see what I couldn't see before. Tracy and her father burned me, but *that* family isn't every family. Archer and I have a working relationship built on professional trust.

My love for London isn't at odds with my career goals. It can live right alongside them. Hell, my relationship with the Hollis family is enhanced because we share the same passions.

I draw in a breath. "All Night Entertainment would love to be in business with you. It sounds like an exciting chance. I'm extremely grateful for the offer, Archer."

"That's great news. We'll get a timeline organized and shoot you a contract by the end of the week. Sound good?"

"Sounds great," I say, extending my hand to shake. "Thank you." But as the words leave my mouth, they don't feel like they're enough. I search for what I really want to say, finding it in my heart. "Seriously, Archer. This opportunity rocks. I'm not sure I deserved this chance after leaving Edge, but I promise I'll make the most of it."

"You bet on yourself, Teddy. That's always a strong play."

But that's not all I need to come clean about. I spent the better part of two weeks trying to have my cake and eat it too. Least I can do is let the guy know how much I appreciate his outlook, but also how much I intend to do right by his sister. "I'm also happy you're being so chill about my dating London. I intend to treat her like she means the world to me, because she does."

"I hope so," Archer says, turning intense. "Because London may be a strong, independent woman who knows her own mind, but she's also my little sister. So if you hurt her—cheat on her, lie to her, forget her birthday—I will end you. Understood?"

"I wouldn't have it any other way," I say as I sip my coffee, slightly afraid of Archer, but mostly thrilled that London has this kind of love in her life already.

* * *

That evening, London and I go on a date to the Greek Theatre, an intimate outdoor music venue nestled in the trees in Griffith Park. As the night winds down, the two of us drunk on music, holding hands under a blanket, getting lost in the stars, Ben Folds plays one of his signature hits, "The Luckiest." I look over at London, and we share a knowing smile.

I flash back to the moment in the market when we heard this number. To when I wondered if I'd have a chance to tell her my philosophy about song timelines.

Now is that chance.

"Did I ever tell you my theory about certain songs?"

"You didn't, but I'm dying to know."

"Sometimes you need to hear a tune one more time and then—boom. It feels brand-new again. Tonight is that night for this song."

"Are you feeling lucky?" she asks, a little flirty, a lot happy.

"No," I say. "I'm feeling the luckiest."

Her grin melts me as she leans in and drops a kiss onto my lips. "What do you know? I feel the exact same way."

I squeeze her a little tighter and nuzzle into her. "I also feel like he wrote this song for us," I whisper to London.

"Maybe he did."

I gently kiss her right behind the ear.

Just the way I did on our first date.

Only this time, it won't be our last.

It'll be the first of many.

Countless, I hope.

From the Woman Power Trio, aka the text messages of London and her two besties, Olive and Emery

London: *sends pic of Mr. Darcy sitting on top of a stack of moving boxes*

Olive: Moving in with Awesome Boyfriend Day. That's the best kind of moving day.

Emery: Yay! So happy for you. I knew he was the one—not just the dog, but the guy. I read enough scripts to know when the storyline is perfect.

Olive: Maybe their romance will become a book, and then we can listen to the Pegasus regale us with the tale of their courtship.

London: And Emery can sell it to Hollywood.

Emery: Dreams do come true! Especially since London found a man who gets all her beautiful sides.

Olive: It's true. He gets her science-geek side and her dance-nerd side.

Emery: And her obsession-with-ice-cream side.

London: He gets my dog fixation too.

Olive: We all do, London. We all do.

EPILOGUE

Six months later

I look good.

Suit, tie, button-down.

Ready to rock it at Temple Israel later today.

After one last glance in the bedroom mirror, I head into the living room dressed for a Saturday afternoon gig. London is curled up with a magazine on the couch, bookended by two fur babies nestled against her thighs.

Those lucky dogs.

I'd be jealous if I didn't have the same access to her.

But I do, so I don't mind sharing with the two pooches I love.

Her eyes sparkle as I enter the room. "Ooh, look at you and your sexy tie."

"Thank you," I say, showing off my look with a spin. "B'nai mitzvah today. Figure two twin boys becoming men is a tie-worthy celebration."

"Well, you look scrumptious."

"Thanks, Lucky. What do you have on tap today?"

"I'm taking these two over to the dog run in a bit. Then, the Burlesque Brunch show I choreographed has two sold-out seatings, so I'm going to run downtown and check them out. Make sure everything looks good."

I grab my phone and keys then head to the couch to give Bowie a high five and Mr. Darcy some scratches.

"Do you need a ride downtown?" I ask. "After I set up, I can come home and give you a lift if you'd like."

"Nope. I'm good," London says with a smile. "I'll take the train. My boyfriend introduced me to the joys of public transit."

"He sounds like a cool guy."

"He's all right," she says, smiling. "Besides, this will give me a chance to look over my notes for André Davies's music video shoot."

"From the little I've seen, you're going to blow them away. Like you always do. Like you did with the show at Edge," I say, since her choreography has turned out to be a huge boon to business. Archer and the partners have been thrilled. I bend down to give her a kiss. "See you tonight, then."

"Mmm," she moans lightly, sending sparks all over my skin. "Indian food and *MythBusters*?" she asks as I head to the door.

That sounds like a perfect evening. "Sexiest Saturday ever."

"It will be if you don't lose that tie. I have plans for that tie. The tie-me-up kind of plans."

Yup, great sex—I'm having it.

Leave it to London to make perfect even better.

ANOTHER EPILOGUE

One year later

It's a picture-perfect Saturday with my woman and our pooches at the dog park. The park is full of the usual weekend crowd, four-legged friends playing in packs while their owners sip coffee or toss tennis balls. This has become a regular highlight of our week.

Only, this morning should be a little out of the ordinary. In a good way, I hope.

In the corner of the park, London gives Mr. Darcy some well-deserved belly rubs, and I scratch Bowie behind the ear to divert his attention from a squirrel in a nearby tree. Petting him has always settled my nerves, and I could use that calm right now.

I steal a glance at London, who's cooing at her favorite little guy. Her love of dogs is yet another thing I adore about the woman of my dreams.

There are so many reasons I love her, and that's why it's time.

Today.

Now.

One more calming breath and I pull the custom-made hedgehog from my hoodie pocket and place it in my pup's mouth.

He truly is man's best friend. "David Bowie, go show London the hedgie," I tell my boy.

Like a dog who's rehearsed this dozens of times, he takes off across the park, rapidly closing the distance to London.

No going back now. But I don't want to go back. With London, the only direction is forward.

I follow the dog, my eyes fixed on my favorite person, the woman who's had my heart for more than a year now.

Bowie reaches London where she's crouched down next to Mr. Darcy, and nudges her elbow with his nose. I take my time making my way over as my pittie sets the hedgie at her feet.

Good boy.

"Aww, Bowie. You brought hedgie to the run today," London says as she picks up the toy. She turns it over, and her eyes land on the large words embroidered on the stuffed animal's chest.

Her lips part.

Even from a few feet away, I hear her breath catch.

She mouths the simple two-word question that could change both of our lives. *Marry me?*

She stands and meets my gaze. My heart pounding

wildly, my fingers tingling, I take one more step then drop to a knee. I don't care if anyone else at the dog park is watching us. At this moment—hell, in every moment since I've met her—the only thing I care about is London.

I speak from the heart—words I haven't written down, born of the feelings that have been running through my mind and soul for months now.

"London Hollis, before I met you, I was focused on my career and assumed that relationships would need to take a back seat for a while. Then I saw you air-guitaring by the bar at the club, and I swear, it was like my focus narrowed to only you, and everything else vanished."

She smiles, and her grin has a life of its own, bursting with emotion. "I remember that night perfectly."

"When I went home, I thought about you all night long. Everything we said to each other. Everything I wished I'd said. Then I saw you at the dog park the next day, and I stopped thinking about how to get lucky and started to feel like maybe I just *was* lucky. Seeing you again. Talking to you. Nerding out over Jane Austen and *90210*, rocking from the 1790s to the 1990s."

"Best dog-park visit ever," she says, her eyes shining with tears.

"It was. Even our dogs liked each other. I love all the things we have in common, but this connection is more than that. You're the most genuine person I've ever met. I admire your passion and dedication to your work. I appreciate the way you listen to me, and I adore the way you care for those dearest to you, humans and animals alike. And every day I've spent with you since the first time we talked, right on this spot, has been the best day of my life."

Her bottom lip quivers, and her hand flies to her mouth. Her reaction spurs me on.

"So now, here I am, at the scene of the Best Dog Park Visit Ever, asking if you'll give me a lifetime to continue getting to know you. What do you say? I don't want to get lucky. I want to have Lucky. Forever. Will you marry me?"

Tears slip down her cheeks as her grin spreads even farther. "Yes, Teddy Lockhart. I would love to marry you."

She drops to her knees, throws her arms around my neck, and plants a fantastic kiss on my lips.

One I will remember for the rest of my life.

But I don't linger, because I have a ring to put on her finger. I dig into my pocket and pull out a small velvet box. We stand as I lift the lid of the ring box. London takes one look at the diamond, then locks eyes with me. "It's so gorgeous."

"So are you." I slide the solitaire on her finger then give her a second or two to stare at it.

Or maybe *gawk* is a better term, and her reaction makes me so damn happy.

"I love this ring, but I love you more, and I love what this means. I can't wait to be married."

"I can't either."

I cup her cheek and kiss my fiancée—a kiss that

lingers until finally we're interrupted by other tongues. Dog tongues, licking our legs.

We laugh, then I look once more at the woman who's going to be my wife, and I grin like the happiest guy ever.

Since I am.

Standing here now, with London in my arms and our dogs by our side, I have one final theory.

I'm exactly where I'm supposed to be.

THE END

Want more from the How To Get Lucky crew? Sign up here to receive a bonus scene sent straight to your inbox!

ALSO BY LAUREN BLAKELY

FULL PACKAGE, the #1 New York Times Bestselling romantic comedy!

BIG ROCK, the hit New York Times Bestselling standalone romantic comedy!

THE SEXY ONE, a New York Times Bestselling standalone romance!

THE KNOCKED UP PLAN, a multi-week USA Today and Amazon Charts Bestselling standalone romance!

MOST VALUABLE PLAYBOY, a sexy multi-week USA Today Bestselling sports romance! And its companion sports romance, MOST LIKELY TO SCORE!

WANDERLUST, a USA Today Bestselling contemporary romance!

COME AS YOU ARE, a Wall Street Journal and multi-week USA Today Bestselling contemporary romance!

PART-TIME LOVER, a multi-week USA Today Bestselling contemporary romance!

UNBREAK MY HEART, an emotional second chance USA Today Bestselling contemporary romance!

BEST LAID PLANS, a sexy friends-to-lovers USA Today

Bestselling romance!

The Heartbreakers! The USA Today and WSJ Bestselling rock star series of standalone!

P.S. IT'S ALWAYS BEEN YOU, a sweeping, second chance romance!

HOW TO GET LUCKY, a sexy romantic comedy co-written with Joe Arden!

CONTACT

We love hearing from readers!

You can find Lauren on Twitter at LaurenBlakely3, Instagram at LaurenBlakelyBooks, Facebook at Lauren-BlakelyBooks, or online at LaurenBlakely.com. You can also email her at laurenblakelybooks@gmail.com

You can find Joe on Twitter at TheRealJoeArden, Face-book at TheRealJoeArden, and Instagram at TheReal-JoeArden or online at TheRealJoeArden.com. You can also email at narratorjoearden@gmail.com

Printed in Great Britain
by Amazon